DEAR ISOBEL

JINNY ALEXANDER

ISBN: paperback 978-1-7353926-1-5
Ebook 978-1-956183-94-8

Any references to historical events, real people or real places are used
factiously. Names, characters, and places are productsof the author's
imagination.

Library of Congress Control Number: 2021950361

Cover Design by Diana TC, triumphcovers.com
Cover photography by Melany Hunt, Le Toi Photography and Digital Arts

First Printing Edition 2022
Published by Creative James Media
Pasadena, MD 21122

DEAR ISOBEL

This book is for my daughter, with love.

CHAPTER ONE

BORROWING CHARLES

*I*t was the best of times, it was the worst of times. I don't want to sound clichéd or dramatic, but these words reverberate in my head on an endless loop. My life has become a cliché, and I can't deny or avoid that fact, however far I bury my head under my pillow or scream at the walls. *A spring of hope.* You can't say fairer than that. Well, I can't. Isobel might say the opposite. Might? Who am I trying to kid?

But this is no tale of two cities; this is a tale of two families, two people who made choices that changed the axis two worlds were spinning on, and a tale of two innocent victims of '*the spring of hope, the epoch of light, and having everything before us*'—all those things working together to ensure two of us made the opposites true for the rest of them. But don't be disillusioned here; we are not descending into a work of future classic and scholarly literature—for this is the story where my life abruptly changed to chicklit, and I don't yet know how to reclaim the high-class literature aspect, except by continuing to borrow Charles. Thanks, Charles—I have taken so much from so many. I am taking your name, as well as your opening lines. What are a few more stolen things along the way? I might as well be hung for a sheep as for a lamb now the path is paved, and the nails are in the coffins, and all those other clichés I could throw in at this point. So, the *'He'* in this story, the '*He'* who changed the world, the *''He'* around whom the events described in these pages orbit —that *'He'*—will now be known as Charles. Shame; it's such a dignified name. Dignity left a long time ago. Shame is paramount.

CHAPTER TWO

DEAR ISOBEL

I hurt too much to think for myself. It's all I can do to get up every morning, yet alone come up with my own coherent thoughts. I have received a text from Isobel, as has James. Although mine contains considerably fewer niceties than the one she sent to James. Charles, it seems, has finally kept a promise, and has told her at last. I reply to her by letter:

Dear Isobel,

You are right to be angry. Yes, I am ashamed. Above everything, I am ashamed of what I have done to you. Some things I won't be able to explain. There is so much I can't understand myself and much less I can expect you to understand. I am not surprised you mention the conversation we had in the summer. That has weighed on me almost more than the rest. I wanted to reassure you that your husband loves you so very much. I know that is true. It was always true. It was such a very long time ago and well and truly over. Although I wanted to talk to you on several occasions, Charles always asked me not to. I told you the truth that day in the summer; I adore you both and my own husband too.

If direct questions had been asked, I would have answered them honestly, but yes, both your husband and I had become 'good' at evading difficult questions. I always told him that if either you or James asked me directly, I would tell the truth, but until that moment, it would be the continuing evasion of questions, scattered with half-truths. You won't be able to understand that you always meant a lot to me, and you certainly won't understand that I had separated 'your' Charles from the Charles I was working with and had grown so close to. They were not the same man . . . somehow.

By the time I had talked to you in the summer, it had been over for a very long time. Yes, I still wanted more than anything to protect you. You, even more than James, because I would never have gotten into such a mess if my marriage hadn't been on crumbling ground anyway. I was clear in my head that my marriage was likely to be finished a long time before Charles and I crossed the uncrossable line. Ironically, since James heard the truth in the last few days. I feel closer to him than I have in years, and, for the first time in a very long time, I believe a huge amount of hope still remains for me to rebuild my marriage. Of course, it's early days yet.

And it is early days. For Isobel, this is the first day of a new life in which everything she knew has changed. For me, it feels more like the last day of everything. My head knows it is early days and that this pain and confusion will pass. It will pass for both of us—for me and for Isobel. My head knows this, but my heart does not.

I don't know how I can make her understand anything at all, when I don't understand anything myself. I do know I must try. I owe her this at least.

Dear Isobel,

It didn't take very long for us to realise just what a huge and destructive thing we had done. That is why it abruptly finished. For the past eighteen months, we have been trying desperately to piece together the remnants of our working relationship. We've had some degree of success and hope but were always so frightened that you and James would find out what we had done to you both. I have always struggled with the knowledge that my business was in your hands. That at any given moment, you could choose to end it. Then, beyond stupidity, I gave you exactly the ammunition to do just that.

I should've walked—not even walked but run like hell— away from the business in spring of last year when I realised we were getting too close. Failing that spectacularly, I should've at least gone a couple of months later when it was over, but I always have believed—and still do believe—so incredibly strongly in the business that I never could go. It has been such a hard fight to keep trying to build the business in the face of all this, and a recession too . . . and yet I had so much passion and belief in the business we had built that I just couldn't leave it.

I know you were always very conscious of how much time we spent together. Charles told me often that you resented that time. For me, after the first six months or so of getting to know each other and finding our feet with our new business partnership, it became a time of confidence, fun, and discovery of who we were and what we could do—to take a dream and make it come true. I had met someone who believed in me, someone I believed in enough to make the business happen. I found myself fitter and healthier than I had ever been. I grew as a photographer and a journalist; I watched Charles grow into so much more than just a farmer. I felt so good about myself and was so happy. It was a strong combination.

You welcomed me into your family with open arms. I felt like I'd found a home in Ireland where I belonged. Our families loved each other, and it was the happiest time of my life. This is no exaggeration, but it was an intoxicating combination. Oh, Isobel, believe me; I don't expect you to realise it yet, but you are not the only one who is feeling this hurt right now. And although I loved him most, I loved you all. I loved you all so much.

Oh, by God, it was intoxicating. Even now, months after, it squeezes the breath out of me, leaves me gasping for air. My heart races, and I remember and remember and remember. I miss them all so much: Isobel, their children, the farm … and Charles. I miss them all, but I miss Charles so very much. It should get easier, with time, but it seems not to. When something feels like everything, will everything else feel like nothing forever after this?

I still have so much I need to say to her. I want her to understand. I want her to understand I hadn't meant to hurt her. I hadn't meant to fall in love, or to destroy my business or our families. I want her to know I couldn't stop it, but that I tried. I know she will only see I didn't try hard enough, but I will keep on trying, because I need her to know how it was.

CHAPTER THREE

TO BE UNDERSTOOD AS TO UNDERSTAND
(AND ABLE TO DO NEITHER)

*D*ear Isobel,
    You know that from the beginning it wasn't all smooth-running. A new business is never easy to build. Forging new friendships, new relationships, and a new partnership are never easy. Running my business from your home was always going to complicate the issue. I did my best to be considerate and thoughtful and to think of you and your family in everything I did. Still, I am quick to lose my temper, and Charles is not always good at communicating, but we carried on, and the good outweighed the bad. Our business seemed to be working . . . even with Ireland spiralling even further into recession. Those difficult times meant so many Irish business were struggling—farmers not least—so people believed in what we were offering and loved our ideas. The feedback was always amazingly positive. We were genuinely helping people find ways to rebrand their own farms and see the recession as a foundation to build from. I loved the lifestyle, the farm, the way my family could be involved and part of it all, and I loved all of you. I love all of you so very much; you and your children have come to mean a great deal

to me. You gave me so much. And I don't know if the inevitable then happened, or if it wasn't inevitable at all and we could've stopped it. I only know we saw it coming, and we did try to stop it. But clearly not hard enough.

You are right to say you treated me like I was someone with integrity. I had also always thought, until this, that I had heaps of integrity. Now, I am faced with knowing what an incredibly horrible thing I have done to you, to James, and our families, to our friendship, and the business. I have destroyed so many people, their lives, and their trust, and I can say without doubt that I never wanted any of this to happen to us. Once the floodgates were open, it was beyond my willpower to hold back the flood. In my head, I separated things, which is not excusable. Please understand I am trying to offer explanation; I know there is no justification, nor any excuses.

Even then, once lines were crossed and the genie out of his bottle, Charles told me often how very much he loved you. I can't tell you why we still did what we did, or why I let it continue; I guess I thought he was kidding himself that your marriage was as good as he said it was. How could it be if he was doing this? Nonetheless, we both knew what we were doing. I, at least, had my eyes open to what it meant for my own future. I thought he did too. I've realised since that I was wrong to think that, and you weren't the only one he wasn't being honest with. If my mistake was to get too close to someone I shouldn't have, then his mistake was to take advantage of that. That said, I must also believe that, at the time, he did mean it and that he didn't intentionally set out to hurt either of us.

I must try to believe this. It is when I allow myself to think maybe he never meant any of it that it hurts the most; those darkest moments when I let myself believe he never cared about me at all, when I want to curl into a small space and disappear. I must believe he meant it. How else will I ever trust my own judgement again? Isobel, it seems, is nothing but angry, so far. Her anger at me is directed through short, hate-filled texts, and her messages to James have quickly moved from the first murmur of empathy with him to attacks on me. Bizarrely, the one that resounds most strongly in my head is the text in which she informs him that she never understood me at all. That, above all, is why I must try so hard to explain it to her and make her understand.

My letters to Isobel are littered with so many clichés. If I had any room left on my pile of shame, I would be ashamed that my life has been reduced to a towering Jenga of clichés. But shame-filled as I am, that is only the very smallest part of what fills me up today, and it is buried far, far beneath the hurt and the grief and the pain. And right on the top of all those feelings is also a strange kind of numbness, laced with ever-flowing tears and bewilderment. How will my days pass now I have nothing left to fill them with? What will I do with the fragments of my ruins?

Each thought triggers another outpouring of questions and explanations I need to bring to Isobel. She is the only one who will understand how I feel about him.

Dear Isobel,

In the past eighteen months or so, Charles and I tried so hard to cling to the fragments of our ruins. We have managed to remain friends on a more acceptable level. It's been hard to share such a dangerous and hurtful secret, and to have become each other's biggest secret. It's necessitated Charles being the only person I could take my anger, hurt, frustration, and guilt out on. This has had its own detrimental impact on the business relationship. Sometimes my hurt and anger have come very close to hate instead, which is, of course, just as destructive. The relief I have felt now that I can share this with James has been enormous. In a ridiculously ironic way though, it has brought me so much closer to him—a consequence I certainly didn't foresee at any stage but am so incredibly grateful for.

I cannot justify or defend any of this. Although I am so very sorry for the hurt, betrayal, and pain I have caused you, I also understand an apology will never put this right. This is something I, you, our families, and our husbands will have with us for the rest of our lives. I am taking one day at a time; picking up scattered pieces of my own marriage. I have no idea where it will take any of us. What you and your family gave to me was amazing. It changed my life in so many ways. What Charles and I have repaid you with is something I will forever have to live with. I just don't know how to do that yet. Many times, over the past few months, it has only been my family who have kept me living with it at all. I cared too much about Charles and the business and clearly not enough about my own family or James. I despise myself for that. I wasn't alone in doing this, but I am so sorry I wasn't strong enough to stop it either. I will miss my business, the land we worked on, and you. I'll miss the lifestyle the business gave to our children. I will also miss, beyond words, one of the closest friends I have ever had. I hope one day you can understand the choices I made were never meant to hurt you or your family. They were selfish and blinkered choices fuelled by excitement, friendship, understanding, and closeness. But beyond the damage done to so many people I love so much, and the guilt for that, I will never regret a huge element of the past four years.

I am not making a lot of sense, I know, but I wanted to try to help you to understand why things happened the way they did. I know I repeat myself too, but that is because I only have the same things to say: please believe, that although I hurt you beyond forgiveness, I didn't intend or plan for it to happen. I believe our feelings are often beyond our control, and maybe that's why I have been so much more of a 'control freak' lately; I have seen the destruction caused by letting go of that control.

I can't understand how this could happen, so I know I can't expect you to. What I do know, without doubt, is this kind of thing does happen. It can happen to the people you least expect. I never thought I was the kind of person who could cheat on either a husband or a friend. I never thought Charles was that kind of person either. He gave me so much, but he has taken so much from me too. My heart breaks for what we are all dealing with now—especially for you and for James who are such good people who deserve so much more than this. I don't know how to make this right.

Charles asked me—told me, in fact—to avoid contact with you, but I feel I, at least, owe you an attempt at explanation. or maybe some of the answers I know you probably need.

So, that was my limited attempt at explaining the inexplicable. There was so much it didn't say, but nothing that would ever say enough. I felt a desperate need to at least give her insight into how it came about. Charles has described it since as a tidal wave, and that is a pretty good description— unstoppable and destructive, sweeping up everyone and everything in its path. How do you ever explain a tidal wave except as a force of nature? I am certain this force of nature was strong enough to make it unstoppable. He came into my life for a reason. It wasn't all bad. Some of it was the best thing that ever happened to me.

CHAPTER FOUR

REALITY CHECK

*C*harles was sure she wouldn't even open the letters and that they would burn on the range with the ashes of every letter I ever wrote him. But, of course, she read them, just as I knew she would.

I'm a woman; she's a woman. I do, at least, know the rules of this one; we *always* read the letters and the texts. I would *like* to not open the texts she sends me. I try not to sometimes. I often don't open them straight away. That first text she sent, for example, as soon as Charles told her our guilty secret, it was never going to be a nice, friendly message or say anything pleasant—no small talk about the weather or the children. I know her texts from now on will say nothing I want to read, but there is always the hope—the desperate, optimistic hope—that one time, just one time, it *will* say exactly what I want to hear. There is also a considerable curiosity as to what is happening in the mind of the person whose life is tangled forever around your own. Besides, as his contact already lessens, it's the closest I can get to him.

So, she opened my letter, and I opened her texted answer.

She's a bit upset. Understandably. Raging, steaming, screaming, and somewhat unhinged would be a more accurate description. She suggests to me that it must feel good to 'purge.' A ridiculous word I have never used in my life, and I am not even sure it applies correctly now. I was careful not to be explicit in the details of the *what,* the *when*, and the *where*. He is clearly sparing no such details himself. I am upset by his sharing of intimate information. Did he also tell her what colour knickers I wore and what noises I made? He may have told her about the times we spent in the office, but did he mention the forest? The fields? The porch? The kitchen? The office was, at least, my staff room, and legitimately somewhere I was supposed to be. What grounds did I ever have to visit her spare room? And did he tell her what we did in there?

I can't decide whether to be offended more by what he has told, or by what he has omitted. I know he has forgotten so much, and I know I have forgotten so little. Either way, I'm not the one who's *'purging'* I won't even tell my own husband these details. Some things are desperately private and should remain so. I am insulted by Charles all over again that he now feels that my sex life is his wife's information. Besides, the details are somewhat irrelevant by this point. By the time we had kissed on more than one occasion, and continued to do so, in her home, in her hallway when she was in the kitchen, on her front porch while our children were inside, what difference did it make how far we actually went? He's clearly told her that I have not confessed to my own husband that we had sex. Her texted rage, kindly offering to ensure James knows I had sex with her husband and where, when, and how, means her husband has told her a different story than the one I have told my own husband.

. . .

Dear Isobel,

Well, really, if that's what you call sex, then no wonder he was bored with you.

By this time, James had already quizzed me to the third degree:

"Hug?" *Yes.*

"Kiss?" *Yes*

"More than once?" *Yes.*

"Intimate touching?" *Yes.*

"Oral?" *Never.*

My life has become a checklist of teenager dating terms. Then we get into words I'm uncomfortable even thinking of, and the questions become more difficult to field. I become increasingly defensive. But, once we've covered pretty much everything, and "Sex?" is the last question left, then, to me, the answer is clearly "No." By the time the list was exhausted to that point, I could only assume that sex must include penetration. So . . . definitely a "no" then. In fact, if we're going for the finer detail, he didn't even take off his boots. So, as I said:

Dear Isobel,

Well, really, if that's what you call sex . . .

I wish we had. It would have felt less incomplete, especially with that being the beginning of the end. After all that time and all his wanting to go to that next stage, it seems that was the defining moment for him in 'a step too far'. Funny, I'd thought that first kiss was the step too far. When he put his hands inside my jeans, a few days later, wasn't that also 'the step too far'? Or later, as we lay half naked in the spare room, endlessly kissing? Surely that was a step too far too? No; despite all that, "If we don't have sex, I will burst," and all that, "I can't be satisfied with just hugs and kisses," it seems that finally coming that close to the real final step too far, was, indeed, the step too far in his mind. Bit bloody late if you ask me.

Dear Isobel.

I have, in fact, told James the whole truth, so, thanks for your kind offer, but you really don't need to. Besides, it seems your detail is not as accurate as mine. It's as if you weren't there while your husband was having relations of a sexual nature with me. Oh, you weren't. It was between Charles and me. I should get therapy? Perhaps I'll see you there.

Of course, I have little doubt that I need therapy, counselling, or someone to talk to. Unlike her, I am not afraid to talk to people. My better friends know me well enough to have guessed what was transpiring many months ago. One or two have followed the unfolding drama with interest to rival a primetime television soap opera. Those who know me best saw what was happening before it even happened. Some offered advice, caution, warning. To most, it was like watching a car crash in slow motion, knowing they were helpless to stop the collision. I will not look for 'real therapy', but neither will I hide this from those who will tolerate listening to it.

Dear Isobel,

You think I need a reality check. I'm not the one who didn't know what's been going on for the last few years. Or the one who seems to think I did this entirely alone.

And then . . . And then! She suggests to me that when I go and get this therapy, then *my* family won't have to deal with *my* self-centeredness, and that I won't continue to hurt everyone anymore.

Dear Isobel,

I think you accidentally sent me a text you meant for your husband.

One day, will she realise his self-centeredness has hurt us *all*—her, me, James, her three daughters, my own two children—but I, in a desperate body count as I claw for moral high ground, can claim one less among my wounded, for I did not hurt Charles like he has hurt me?

Dear Isobel,

Charles was the one who said he wanted to have it all. I always knew I couldn't. Besides, my family ARE dealing with it quite well, thank you. I don't see James hurling abuse at you or Charles, or at me either. It is somewhat ironic that the marriage I accepted I would have to sacrifice is the one that will survive. Do you think Charles thought he'd get to keep his marriage and have his fling? At the time, I never expected to keep my marriage.

When Charles was putting his arms around me and kissing me like he loved me, yet still telling me how much he loved her, why then, *why* was he kissing me at all?

CHAPTER FIVE

VULNERABLE

I think we all understand that at pushing forty years old, Facebook is not a good place to spend too much time—but too much time I spend there regardless. I will argue it is a good place to see photos of your loved ones who live far away, and to see a photo of what your distant cousin had for breakfast on the second Tuesday of March, and that lots of people have very cute kittens/babies/hats. Mostly, however, I just use it to chat to friends when the children or James might be too close for me to talk audibly on the phone. And so, chat I do, and without the chat of my friends, I would be insane, if not dead, by now.

I am fortunate to have a friend willing to listen to me, and who knows me well enough to know what I need her to say. She is there for me to spiel my life to at any hour of any day. The similarity of her own business means she has mentored and advised us along the way. She, too, has turned a failing farm into something new. She has met and liked Charles and has known our secret for a while.

There were a few days of limbo between my telling James, and Charles telling Isobel. These were strange days where we bounced between everything being fine and nothing being fine. There was some relief in James finally knowing, and the weekend after I told him was spent happier in each other's company than we had known for some time. James's birthday fell that week, and, against all odds, we were still spending it together as a family. I'm not a completely insensitive bitch; I didn't *choose* to tell him just before his birthday. He was the one who finally cornered me and asked me outright, the Friday before. I didn't ever *choose* to tell him at all. We'd spent much time over the weekend talking to each other, and I felt closer to him than I had in years. These days are easy to recount. Never mind the aforementioned hypothetical second Tuesday of March, and my cousin's breakfast; instead, I can rewind straight to the second Thursday in September with graphic clarity and the help of not having immediately deleted the conversation I had with Anna late into that evening:

Oh, Anna, somehow, I've had a pretty good week. It's James's birthday today, and we're doing it together against all the odds . . . We're talking to each other, and I feel closer to him than I have in years. Yes, I know it's early days yet! But now Charles is in pieces and thinks it's time to pull the plug on the business . . . I have never seen him hurting like this . . .

It was a strange few days—that period when James knew, and Charles knew that James knew. I was still maintaining my determination that Isobel didn't need to know at all, and Charles was simply worrying about who would tell her first —him or James.

Anna replied instantly. I was pleased she was there in real time; it's so much easier to talk without the long pauses we have sometimes while I wait impatiently for her to be online.

What do you mean, he is in pieces? I am so pleased that

you and James are communicating honestly and caring for each other. Poor Charles . . . it's a car crash, the whole thing. Isn't it amazing that, for the first time in a long time, you are slightly less vulnerable than him? Weird really.

It was weird indeed.

Weird, definitely, **I** replied. *And Charles is probably right that we can't really carry on, but we've been making such great plans, and I have nearly finished the beautiful new magazine pages . . . and we just committed to loads of new ideas for next year, and I can't imagine not having him in my life, and . . .*

I ran out of words. I didn't know how to tell her what I wanted to say, because the only person I wanted to say it to was Charles. Anna and I chatted for a while longer as she tried to hold me together.

Maybe, just maybe, it will work out in a way that you can continue . . . And what do you mean, he's in bits? About what, in particular? I must go in a minute . . . Would love to hear more. Will try to call or Facebook later.

And then Anna was gone, but I answered her anyway.

It's James's birthday, so I won't be chatting later. Tomorrow's better. Basically, Charles fears Isobel finding out, and the deception he's been living with for the past few years coming crashing down . . . broken down into exact bits though, it's all the things that Isobel finding out will change for him/me/us/the business.

XXXXX Love you.

So many things worry us both now.

It has been a constant struggle to keep the business going when we are torn between loving and hating each other and have been living with the worry of James and Isobel discovering what we have done. It's been hard not to let our readers and our followers guess that something is wrong too.

Our business has always been in Isobel's hands, and now we have given her the reason to end it for us. I should have quit then and walked away with the remnants of friendship between Charles and me. I should've walked away that day, the second Thursday in September, while Charles was distraught, and I was the stronger one—while I could offer comfort, support, and ongoing friendship. I should have walked away with a hug and tears of sadness. I should never have waited so long and let it become an ending of tears of rage, with all hope of friendship dead. I could wish for hindsight above all else, but then hindsight might have stopped us doing what we did, and I can't regret that at all.

Anna and I resumed our conversation a few days after James's birthday when she popped into my chat window with: *Are you there, honey?* I'm not entirely sure where else she thought I may be those days. I was floundering and rootless. I no longer had certainty of welcome at my place of work, as I no longer had certainty as to when Isobel would know what the rest of us now knew. It had only been a few days since I admitted everything to James, but it already seemed as if for Charles, this changed everything again. So, yes, Anna, I am here.

Well, fill me in a bit more, she wrote, *How are you all doing, and I take it you are doing the tourism fair this weekend—together?*

For among all our other plans, we had committed to working offsite the following weekend, to promote our book, and we needed to rally staff and marquees, and finalise advertising, promotional materials, and press coverage.

Well, we were on Wednesday, when everything seemed to be going okay, and he seemed fairly positive about the business, and we were planning for next year's schedule and everything, and so on Thurs morn, when, as you know,

I woke up feeling okay about the world in general, and it was James's birthday, and I had an 'at home' day ahead of me . . . I tailed off and hit Send to give her time to read that before I continued.

She sensed hesitation and typed back quickly,

I think I hear a 'but' on its way?

I relayed Thursday's events, relieved to have her as an outlet to spill my thoughts to.

And I made a cake, and walked the dog, and got on with the final edit for the latest article and was really pleased with how it was coming together, so I sent Charles a text to ask how he is and has he any alterations to make to my layout ... I hit Send again, breaking up the spiel of typing, then continued. *Sorry, am aware that sometimes my messages are too long, and I must wait for you to catch up.*

I sent this, then paused, knowing she would be enjoying the dramatisation of my day. I admit, sending the text to Charles was an excuse. I knew, already, he wouldn't have had changes to make to the layout; we'd finalised it all on the Monday evening. We had spent the evening in the comfort of his kitchen, working together at the farmhouse table, like we spent so many Monday evenings. Our working weeks were accustomed to beginning over chat, a glass of wine, casual intimacy, and his children drifting in and out around us while Isobel was at her fitness class. But I sent him the text anyway, because I needed to add, "How are you today?" After all, above all else, we were friends, and I care how he is. He had phoned me straight back.

So, then he gets the text and phones me, I told Anna. I pressed Send, then I paused again. I grasped at small moments of enjoyment through this; keeping Anna on tenterhooks while waiting for the story to unfold were the brightest moments I could find, during those in between days.

—and says . . . I sent this, but the cursor flashed to tell me she was typing, so I waited for her to catch up before continuing. Nothing arrived, so I kept going.

Sorry, it said you were typing, so I was waiting.

No, I'm just waiting for the cliff-hanger!

(That's not what he said, of course!), I typed, dragging it out.

Of course. So, what did he say?

What he had actually said had been an unexpected blow after the 'show-must-go-on' attitude we'd been adopting all week. I was happily convincing myself that we would continue as normal, and that James knowing about what we'd done would alter nothing for the future, since he seemed willing to believe it was in the past.

He said he really can't see a way to continue, and we should end it, I typed to Anna, through the tears blurring my vision. I got up to find tissues, but none were left, so I had to get a wodge of toilet roll instead. I was glad she couldn't see me right then, although she had already listened to me crying to her on the phone many times.

Have you seen him since? she wrote. **If James has coped, Isobel certainly could do with a bit of reality, I'd think.**

I told her I was quite stunned, on the strength of Monday evening's "count me in" about the weekend, and the good day we'd had together on the Wednesday, planning for the future of the business, so I didn't listen. I'd cut off the conversation with him and resumed baking James's birthday cake. Undeterred by my avoidance of his words, Charles had called again, and I didn't listen some more. Then he sent a message, asking we could talk about it, and I said, *No, we can't.* Then he sent a couple of *I don't know what to do* texts, and I'd never known him to seem so vulnerable. As I relayed all this to Anna, crying properly by now, my heart ached for him.

While James was relieved and calmer since he now knew for certain what he had suspected for a while, albeit still upset and confused by my actions, the knowledge that our secret was out had hit Charles hard—for fear of Isobel finding out rather than for fear of losing me—and he was in pieces. He felt the only possible thing to do would be to end our business. I felt it was all I had left. I felt it may be all I had left of him. He was distraught and confused and terrified. I had never seen him hurting like that. For once, it seemed I was less vulnerable than him.

Inevitably, my heart melted for him once more, and I abandoned my pretence of domestic bliss, left the birthday cake cooling, and went to the forest to find him.

So, I went to the forest to find him, and it probably isn't a good idea to surprise a man using a chainsaw, I relayed to Anna.

Vulnerability is always cute, she answered.

And now I'm sitting here laughing out loud, although it's not funny!! I replied, as the funny side temporarily eclipsed the sadness. I blew my nose inelegantly and loudly, to try to make room for the humour.

I am too, she typed, *but did he really have a chainsaw, or was that for effect?*

He did really have a chainsaw; he was clearing a new pathway to the site where he hoped to have the new cabin built before Christmas and ready to use the following spring. It took a few minutes before he saw me standing there and cut off the power. He kept hold of the saw, holding it across his body like a shield—or a weapon. I think he thought I would see he was busy and go away again. The lines on his face and the darkness under his eyes were more pronounced under the shadows of the trees. I stood, looking at him, until he lowered the saw to the ground and sat on one of the freshly hewn stumps. I stayed out of reach, afraid to move close enough to fall into his arms. He had felled a thick tree trunk to lie horizontal across the ground, like a park bench, so I scrambled up to sit on it, one leg hanging over each side, and turned towards him. Stuck for words of my own, and afraid to hear his, I wished I'd brought tea with me—something to give him and something to hold my hands still.

But anyway, I told Anna, *he put down the chainsaw, and I tried to listen, and he is in pieces and doesn't know where he's at and doesn't see how Isobel won't find out, and he doesn't know how can we keep running the business. He feels he can no longer come to my doorstep now that James knows what he's done, and I do understand that, for how can I go to his place if Isobel knows what I've done to her? And if I can't go there, how can I work?*

With a quick tap of a button on her end of the conversation, she was gone, for the drama of my life was still a secret on so many levels, and someone had arrived in her house. I continued the conversation in case she was only temporarily gone and needed to know if the ending was happy.

He did have a chainsaw and was using it to cut a new pathway in the forest. She was not there to answer, but I carried on, making up an ending for this story. *Oh no, now you'll never know if he picked the chainsaw back up . . . Guess you're not coming back just now. So … then the chainsaw erupted into life of its own, cut off his head, and I danced on his bleeding body, singing, "That's what you deserve, you cheating bastard" Goodnight xxxxx*

I hit Send, wishing and wishing this was all nothing more than a made-up story. Of course, it isn't, and I needed to remind her of that, in case we forget this is real, so I added a codicil.

Oops, slipped into a little fantasy there, I think. Really, it is heart-breaking to see both the men in my life so distraught. I was once again left to my own thoughts, slipping into the fantasy of my mind, which runs away with the story and either puts everything right or kills us all.

Anna and I frequently talk on the phone, for she keeps me reassured of my sanity, and makes me laugh at myself, at him, at Isobel, and at the whole situation I got myself into. I feel bad I inflict my trauma on her so often, but I always feel better once I've talked to her. She is on my side. She may not believe I have done a good thing, but she never judges. Talking to Anna, I can turn my mountain back into a molehill, and make my crisis just a drama.

I need to interject some seriousness too though.

Hi, Anna, me again. Have you any work for me out there!? XXX

Because, at the end of the day—although I am clearly not Victim Number One in the sorry saga of the way I destroyed our lives—I am, nonetheless, the one who has no work anymore. I have mouths to feed and bills to pay, and what will I do with my life now, when, I still had a business on the Monday after James's birthday, and by that Tuesday morning, it was gone quicker than water in an emptying bathtub?

CHAPTER SIX

DELUSION

*T*oday, I stumble into Fairyland.

We are walking on the bog again today, my dog Jess and I, and there at the bottom of the oak tree, is a whole gathering of those storybook mushrooms—red and white-spotted toadstools. I am not so deluded that I will tell you there are little doors or windows and pixies dancing around the place. But it is a magical distraction. For a fleeting moment, my hands go automatically to where my camera usually hangs around neck, bouncing against my chest, like my heartbeat, but then I remember how everything I see through its lens now is Charles, so I have, as usual since we fell apart, left it at home. These days, the pounding I feel against my chest is only the frantic heaving of my heart as it breaks. The sight of the fairyland toadstools makes me reconsider that whole issue of how deluded I really am.

Isobel texted me again yesterday, and her messages left me shaken, upset, lonely, and sad. But now, in the cold light of day, and a chat with Anna to share it, it looks more like everything in those messages was nothing but a mirror she could hold up to her own face.

Dear Isobel,

Er . . . I was leaving you alone. You just texted me to say, 'leave you alone,' but I have had no contact with you for weeks. Who's not leaving who alone?

I am not only leaving her alone, but I feel both physically and mentally quite alone all the time now. Here, in the middle of the bog, with only my dog and my thoughts for company, I should welcome her contact. I wonder if she, too, feels lonely and alone and this is why she feels the need to contact me. I saw him, earlier in the week, and this, presumably, is considered 'not leaving her alone', but we had business matters to deal with.

Dear Isobel,

I can't believe Charles even told you I slapped him. Did he come running home crying? I'm flattered, really, I didn't think he'd even felt my feeble girly slap. Did he tell you I had to do three of them, just hoping I'd eventually hear that cracking noise you get in films when the girl slaps the boy, and it really hurts (but only hurts his face and never her hand)? Well, I am embarrassed to admit it didn't even hurt my hand. But, if you are serious about bringing me up for assault, then at least let me kick him really hard in the balls. If only I could find them.

I am shocked he told her I slapped him, but I am even more shocked by her response. Perhaps she is only jealous that, once again, I did to her husband what she wanted to do herself. There have been so many times already when I should've slapped him. The most obvious, if not necessarily the first, being after (not before, oh God, not before, I wouldn't have missed it for the world) that first delicious kiss. A good, hard slap that could've stopped all this before it started. Although, if I'm honest, the kiss was not the start either. Things had started a long time before that.

Dear Isobel,

***If I'd slapped him the first time he tried to kiss me,
would you have thanked me then?***

A good, hard slap eighteen months ago when he first told
me our affair was over could have been a good plan too, but I
was still trying to be calm and business-like then, so I
remained restrained—calm and restrained apart from the
endless tears, anyway. The hope of it not really being over
back then maybe kept me from 'assault' at that stage too.

I should have slapped him so many times when his
nonchalance enraged me as I worked for our business whilst
his enthusiasm for it was so clearly slipping away, despite his
reassurance that he still loved it as much as I did. For him, I
know now, the cloud of Isobel finding out our secret was
becoming too heavy for him to bear, and this fear
overshadowed any passion he had for anything else.

But the slap to which Isobel refers in her text finally came
when his refusal to help me wind up our business accounts in
the midst of my own despair had left me floundering and
unable to complete the necessary paperwork without his
input. The days have rolled on, and September has become
October, and I am beginning to know with absolute certainty
that I have fallen into the pages of some chicklit saga or
Victorian melodrama. I am waiting with cliffhanging, page-
turning, bated breath to see if a happy ending is still to come.
For now, it feels easiest to deal with one day at a time, but I
find it hard to do that when other people want to throw a
different day at me to the one I'm trying to deal with. We are
no longer working, but there are still things to sort out. Once
again, his delusion and head-in-the-sand attitude has left me
trying to pick up the pieces. His refusal to end our beautiful,
hard-earned, increasingly successful business in any way
other than a flat, overnight decision to never talk to me again

leaves me to deal alone with banks and accountants, receipts and bills. He met me at my gate on Monday to hand me a jumbled bag of loose papers and a cashbox, which I dropped in the confusion of his proximity. He tried to help pick it all up, but it was far too late by then for help. So, yes, I slapped him.

I am only sorry it didn't hurt him like he has hurt me.

Dear Isobel,

James says Charles should count himself lucky that I hit him before he did.

Isobel and James both, in fact. They should both be grateful I have now set the face-slapping precedent. They can join a queue to be next in line to slap him. Yet, she has the cheek to threaten to report me for assault!

Dear Isobel,

Assault? Well anytime you'd like me to go through the ways in which I feel assaulted by your husband, let me know.

In my long-overdue wisdom, I know it is better to say nothing, and I should not be sending her these angry messages.

But I cannot stop myself.

Dear Isobel,

Why the hell are you not delighted I slapped him? I hope you have slapped him too by now.

So, there we are, Jess and I, on this bright October day, walking through the bog. Among all the bleak beauty of the bog casting off summer and preparing itself for its winter landscape is a strong stench of rotting. I find myself recalling a conversation with Charles some time back, when he announced the best way to dispose of a body is to dump it in the bog. In the solitude of my thoughts, my mind makes a leap from the here and now, to my becoming the next four-thousand-year-old Bog Body. I consider whether there'd be any of me left to identify the period in which I had lived (and died), and how quickly would the studs in my ears rust to nothing? I wonder whether I am wearing any synthetic clothing that might disintegrate slowly (no) and think what a shame my new €200 walking boots will be wasted. But, if I am strangled with the dog chain which is currently hanging around my shoulders on the end of the lead, while Jess runs free, then maybe that would be a good clue for future archaeologists.

I wonder if Jess would become Loyal Dog and sit by my body forever until her own corpse rots beside my bog-preserved remains, or will she become Superhero Lassie Dog and run home to raise the alarm, and my sleeping, just-home-from-night-shift husband? Or will she just revert to Not-Having-Lived-With-Us-For-Long Dog, and run off after the sheep in the next field, and that will be that? I suspect probably the last option. Jess has, in fact, disappeared while my mind has wandered. I call her, and I call her, but my calls disappear into the wind, and nobody can hear me cry, and nobody responds to my calls. I love the loneliness of this bog, where it seems I am the only person ever to come here, but equally, its loneliness gives me too much time alone with my own thoughts, and now I have scared myself into feeling absurdly nervous as I walk back along the bog lane towards home, hoping Jess will catch me up when she remembers I am here.

Usually, I am only nervous walking on the road that Isobel drives on to get to work—the road that goes past my front gate—but now my mind has taken off into a crime scene story where, somehow, Isobel knows I am at the bog, and she knows it is secluded at this time of year and no one will 'just pass by'. In my runaway mind, she knows it is far, far away from the road so no one will see a thing, and as I'm walking towards the proper road, I am convinced she will be driving towards me down this muddy bog track. I try to shake off those thoughts by picking a blackberry, but they are not as sweet and juicy as they usually are, and it is just something else that leaves a bitter taste in my mouth.

Reality catches up with me as I near the end of the bog lane. I realise, in that lovely new car she recently bought that Charles told me they really couldn't afford, and he didn't want anyway, she will never venture down the bog track. The lovely new car is the same reason why she won't run me off the road when she swerves towards me if I pass her when I am driving. But none of this stops me feeling like I must always watch my back when I am walking. I have whiled away many uncomfortable hours of dog-walking, trying to second-guess the situation that will inevitably one day arise; we will certainly pass, one of these days. Will she ignore me, or run me down? Would she run my dog down too? What if my daughter is with me, as is often the case? Once she has run me down, would she stop? To help? To kill? Every possible scenario has played in my mind, including the ones where he is there too. Sometimes he helps her; sometimes he helps me. But, back in reality, I'm beginning to realise he is proving himself to be so spineless, so happy to be controlled by her, that I'm sure he would help her and not me. Or at least not hinder her, or throw himself between us.

My newfound time-filler of working with the clay equipment I salvaged from the farm is proving to be therapeutic. It gives me something to focus on and take out my anger on, so, as I walk home, I consider the things I will make next. The clay is a useful distraction, particularly in the absence of much hope lingering in my polytunnel, where I spent much of the last few weeks, pretending to tidy and harvest, but mostly just crying into the dead tomato plants. We did manage to harvest enough last-dregs tomatoes to make tomato sauce for seven separate meals, which is a small achievement. I wish the tunnel would not make me think of better times and the fun of buying them—one for my garden and one for Charles's garden —and sharing plans and plants and seeds and dreams. They proved a valuable addition to our articles and video-diaries, and were popular with a whole new audience, as well as our existing audience. Now, as autumn gives way to the long pastel shades of winter frosts and bare earth, I will document one last dying edition. This swansong will, for obvious necessity, be me alone. I will record it alone with a camera that shakes not for effect, but for lack of control over my own limbs, and, undoubtedly, a voice that shakes as well. I don't want to do it, but I know I must face it soon. Our 'public'—yes, it still sounds ridiculous to call them that, but that is what our audience has become—our public are owed an explanation for the abrupt cease of our broadcasts and updates. Nonetheless, I know I must be the deluded one when all I think of when I look out at my broccoli patch is him. I hope caterpillars and slugs eat all his crops, and all his potatoes get blight. When I get home from my walk with Jess, I will throw myself into making clay, or tidying up the garden, while the day is nice.

For today, the sun is finally shining, and, although the ground is saturated enough to have sunk my dead body into the bog in seconds, it feels good to have the sun on my face for a change. It is hard to pick up the pieces of a broken life when the days are grey, rainy, and persistent with foggy drizzle. It is so much easier to find focus on a sunny October morning like this. I turn my face to the warmth and shut my eyes against the orange glow, resting for a moment against a field gate. It is while I force myself to relax and enjoy the sun's rays that Jess reappears suddenly behind me, making my heart jump, as if someone who wants to kill me was about to stab my back.

It has become a strange twist to be despising Isobel, and feeling that she must, as Anna has been suggesting for months, be living in Cloud Cuckoo Land. I understand her anger, her hurt, and her feelings of betrayal, but I do not understand her lack of understanding. I must be very selfish to even consider myself a victim too, as they keep pointing out to me—Charles and Isobel both. I do know I am not one of the poor innocent victims of what we did, but I would be more than willing to spell out to her, once again, the reasons why I am hurting too. Surely even someone who shoots herself in the foot can still feel the pain?

They have also both been telling me for months I am a control freak. I know she had suspected, for a while, that something was going on, but as Charles and I had both assured her it wasn't, she had chosen to believe that. It wasn't really a lie, by the time she asked us. However, she had been less friendly towards me for some time, and my mood must have been noticeably disagreeable as I stamped and stropped my way through so many of my days after Charles had broken off our affair. So, that I had become something of a control freak may be true, but right now, I'm not the one who is dictating who my husband can or can't speak to or take calls or texts from. I'm not the one who demands use of her husband's phone to send her emotional rants from. I'm not the one who included the instruction, *Do not reply to this,* in the last message.

Dear Isobel,

Okay, I won't reply, but did you say I am the control freak?

I am impressed to finally discover in myself the ability to not need the last word.

Well, not out loud, at least, so I don't press 'Send' this time.

She thinks I am the only one who is deluded. She must be deluded to think that.

CHAPTER SEVEN

FUNERAL

*O*h, the irony of it all. For the last fourteen months or so (June of last year until the September just gone, to be precise), I have been holding on to memories of what had happened already. Charles told me over and over to let it go. Yet, now, only now, as we roll towards winter and everything is out in the open, do I want to look forward, just at the same time everyone else needs to look back. How's a girl to move on, when suddenly the rest of the world needs to rehash the past?

My desperation and recurring barrage of *'Why?'* and *'How?'* and *'Did it ever mean anything at all?'* have annoyed the hell out of Charles for months. His inability to realise I needed to keep questioning until I found some answers, and my inability to realise he just needed to move on, was echoed by the same pattern at home. James's neediness to get my attention and love and acknowledgement was driving me completely insane. It was this constant smothering that made him unappealing. I could see it reflected in my behaviour towards Charles; after he finished our affair, I was making myself equally unappealing to him, but, as everything else that has gone before, I was incapable of controlling it. How can I be labelled as a control freak but equally so unable to control my own behaviour? Isobel is right; I need therapy.

In the great scheme of curveballs, I find it easy enough now to pass off Isobel's frantic ranting texts as her need to vent her rage and temporary insanity. I steam and sulk and cry when I read them, but after an hour or so—all right, a day or two—I have all but forgotten them and moved on. I understand her need to rage at me. When James does it though, it's another story. He wants answers to questions I'm trying to not exactly forget, but certainly want to remember with less clarity. He is doing no less than I have done for the past fourteen months, but I am now the Charles in the situation. Today, I even find myself using the same line Charles yelled at me, one day near the end, "Park it; let it rust." I was so upset when he said it to me, but now I fling the words at James, as if they are something else of Charles's I will use to wound my own husband. Since last June, I have been spending my days wondering how to move on, and now I am being pushed to recall the past instead. It is so fresh and so new to James and Isobel that I must remember they are now living through similar feelings of bewilderment to those I had last summer, but I cannot help them. I cannot help Isobel because she wants to hate me. I cannot help Charles because he wants to pretend I don't exist. I cannot help James because I am trying to move on, and if I must help him, it stops me from moving forward.

I spent last winter in the ultimate depths of despair. My Christmas with James culminated in "I think we should separate." My New Year's was a fabulous riot of "I'm leaving." "You're leaving." "This can't work anymore." My New Year's resolution was about as close as planning to throw myself under a bus as anyone can get. Which is a particularly challenging resolution if that particular *anyone* happens to live in rural Ireland where there are no buses. On any given day, I could find myself wondering if I would die outright if I drove into that tree, that wall, that field, that river. Every day, I was saved only by a flashing premonition of my children sobbing by graveside—a macabre vision of my tearful children clinging to each other as if they were all they had left in the world; saved too, by the further damage I would inevitably do to James, leaving him to be the surviving parent to the grieving children whose mother had chosen to do herself in. I suspected, in my dreary daydreams, Charles would probably not even stand by my graveside, but dance on the grave later when the ground was settled and the crowds dispersed.

I should have been beginning to recognise the clues from those insightful graveside mind flashes from nearly a year ago; Charles would never do something so emotional as cry at my funeral. God no, that might let people think he cared, lead to awkward questions, and let the cat out the bag. Why would he be upset at the loss of someone who was, after all, only their business partner and friend? To be seen wiping a tear from his eye would surely lead to the neighbours talking: "Shock;" "Horror;" "See how upset he is? He must've slept with her." To Charles, this would be what they would be thinking, for surely no rational person could cry over 'just a friend'?

By that dark winter a year ago, it was already half a year since our affair ended, but it still felt fresh with longing and the hint of it not being truly over. Whilst Charles and I were the only keepers of the secret, I could cling onto hope that the simmering embers would be rekindled. Again and again, I visualized an amazing fantasy of graveside possibilities. In my morbid daydreams, I was always buried in the little village church despite it being disused now. It has a far more dramatic, hilltop setting than the larger modern one down the road. In the village church setting of my tragic fantasies, black coats billowed dramatically against a stormy backdrop whilst a multitude of weeping mourners huddled under black umbrellas, clutching red roses, and wailing. The church morphed with the artistic license of a daydreamer, and beautiful, twisted, black wrought iron railings and gates were everywhere, and crows calling mournfully. Although it was winter, the backdrop was always black stormy skies—never pretty—and a gentle snowfall. Blood-red roses entwined those imaginary railings. and the trees were heavy with ravens flown in straight from Edgar Allan Poe. It was beautiful, but bleak. I had, through this winter of discontent, become a Victorian gothic novel.

It seems like a welcome respite from my chicklit present. However, it is to chicklit my life returns, as, over time, I pull myself from this depression, only allowing it to surface once a month, where those around me can label it as PMT instead.

The real point of that depressing side-tracking did, of course, originate in the reasons why I can't help James to move on. I am, in all truthfulness, terrified of going back there. Much as I am not happy to be the main character in a chicklit novel, I really don't want to become a victim in a horror movie either. I will not place my children in the starring roles of Motherless and Bereft, their lives ruined by the sins of their parents. Well, one of their parents. Me. I really am selfish; Isobel is right with that observation. I will not have my life be made into a horror film, because I don't want to look like the bad guy at my own funeral.

But I *am* the bad guy. I can't pretend I'm not; even in this story, I have become it. I want to turn these pages really quickly to reach the happy ending—or at least reach a chapter where it turns around for the better, and that is the problem with being fourteen months ahead of James with my grief and my recovery. It is also the problem with being fourteen months ahead of Isobel, who may kill me yet, which I presume would still not even bring a happy ending to her own side of the story.

She may decide the risks are worth it.

CHAPTER EIGHT

42

oday sees me waiting for the post—a strange delivery of one hundred and twenty second-hand golf balls. I wonder if they will be boxed, or loosely tied in an untidy brown paper package so when I pull undone the string, it will send them cascading to the floor. I will spend hours on my hands and knees, chasing them around, until I am sure I have them all, and every time I try to hold them all, some will certainly fall again. I will spend my day making futile attempts to gather all the parts and hold them secure to turn them into something real and sustainable and tangible. And then, even at the next stage of their career, they will become felted juggling balls, a constant whirl of colour and chaos, to throw into someone else's life.

I can't decide whether I am allowing myself to become engulfed by my own chaos or whether my desire to create is a desperate search for therapy—therapy through art, if you like. I know a commercial viability could grow from my self-imposed art therapy, and it is indeed a market I could tap into, or seek employment in, but to be either in need of art therapy or to use it for commercial gain is hard to admit. I know in my own reality, with my thumping of clay and relentless jabbing of barbed needles into wool for felting, I'm only a step from voodoo dolls and black magic, never mind any form of therapy. So, overall, I won't see this new activity as any level of therapy, just an instinct to survive, balanced with a barbaric need to work out anger and frustration on a physical level. It is nothing but viciousness, caused by the constant throb of hurt, and only very thinly disguised as art. What I do know, however, is I must carry on. At least by doing something with my time and my hands I can distract my mind and my thoughts and forget about life for a while. The total focus of *making* is enough to give me a short break from the sheer difficulty of *being*.

These things I am filling my time with are included in the spoils of the war; amongst the activities Charles and I explored as part of our 'Things to do on a farm that don't smell or bite' feature, we offered a series of pottery workshops and textile crafts, in a beautifully converted wood-beamed barn a short walk from the forest cabins. I brought what materials I could salvage with me, and Isobel unceremoniously delivered the rest one Saturday morning in late September, dumped on my doorstep on a day she knew I was away from home. I am left with pottery equipment—including a working kiln, and *that* was no fun to move in a hurry—many bags of soft merino wool, a whole lot of paint, and a broken heart. I guess the pottery equipment and the wool might be more useful to my immediate future than this pain in my heart.

By the end of the week, I have made twenty-five clay nativity figures, nine flat clay angels, seven games, and four sets of felt juggling balls. It seems strange that the therapy I find in thumping clay leads me to making angels. I wonder now if I still believe in a God. The God I believe in believes in love, but he's not so good at telling me how to deal with loving two people at the same time. I am making angels for nothing other than the mercenary act of knowing many people are out there who need to believe in angels and will buy them for Christmas.

I am also struck by the mockery of making games, especially the Snakes and Ladders sets I'm working on, when no fun exists in my life anymore. I'm proud of how they are progressing. As my mind wanders from the intense focus of drawing the patterns in the clay, I notice every ladder has a snake, and every snake has a ladder. Somehow, the players always persist, hoping the ladders will triumph. They aim for the top, whatever it takes. Can this be the same in the game of life? I will paint my snakes in the brightest glazes I have, because the snakes are always there, but sometimes they are the fun parts. Sometimes, it seems the snakes are the ladders for a time, bringing you to places you didn't expect to go. Then, just when you least expect it, they show their true colours and swallow you whole or drip venom into your life for evermore.

It is better to keep my mind firmly on the job at hand, as I suddenly notice my numbers are wrong. Is it another joke that the mistake I have made is I've drawn in two number '42's— the Ultimate Answer to Life, the Universe and Everything? It's been years since I read *Hitchhiker's Guide to the Galaxy,* but that much I remember, and now I have two 42's, which must prove there is always an option in life, and sometimes it seems you can travel on two paths simultaneously. I wish, I wish, I wish. And suddenly, my mind is wandering again.

So, here I am, making games, making juggling sets, and

making angels. Day after day, as October limps on, I pass the time by trying to juggle the combination of moving on and looking back. I try to get the ups and downs in an order for the ups to win, and all the while, I'm desperately wanting to believe in things stronger and more powerful than me.

It's hard to be motivated in this bizarre, new *at-home* life I've been thrown into, when it's not a sunny and bright autumn day today, but as dull and depressing as an Irish winter. Last week's temper-cleaning of my house has given me windows I can see through, but what is the point of clean windows if the world outside is grey? I will paint my ladders grey and the snakes in bright colours, because it is the snakes that distract us the most.

I think it was the snakes that kept me awake last night. Today I must take my daughter to their house for her French lesson. For the last few months, all the Monday evenings Charles and I pretended to work, our children would be ensconced in our office space, across the yard, being tutored in French by a willing local post-grad for extra rent money. I don't know how long we can sustain this attempt at keeping one small sliver of 'normality' in the children's lives. I don't know how Isobel has allowed it to continue, but I hope it is her love for our children and her need to hide the truth from them that allows this weekly foray into her territory. There's a new ground rule; I am not allowed inside. I am nervous already, although I know neither Charles nor Isobel should be there. She will be absent because she will be at her fitness class. He will be absent because he will be hiding. I am nervous that maybe she will be home regardless—late to leave, early home, a cancelled workout session, or just a need to confront me when she knows I may be the one to do the carpool journey tonight. I hope he'll be there, but I also hope he won't. I hope he will be civil and invite me in—of course, I can't go in, but we could sit on the porch and make polite conversation and pretend we are strangers who have barely met. We could discuss the stormy weather and ask politely about the children.

I could look at his face and know how he is.

I hope he won't be there because none of that will happen. If he is there, he will hide inside the house, and I will be rejected again. I miss my friend, above everything. I am also nervous I will meet Isobel on her driveway, where it is too narrow to pass, and I will have to stay calm and reverse forever while I know she is trying to control herself enough to not ram my car with her own, or to stop me and claw out my eyes. Or worse. Much worse, all in front of my daughter.

Someone once said that in every relationship, one person always loves more. This, I know now, is true. The snakes will keep me awake again tonight; for whichever way the evening goes, it will not be how I want, and I will relive it repeatedly in my mind, both as it was and as I wished it.

CHAPTER NINE

DISTANCE

*T*ell me often enough I am angry, and I certainly will be, if I wasn't already. Ask me often enough what's wrong, and, eventually, there will be something. James is smothering me again, and I am upset by this, because I think the kiss I give him as he leaves for work is passionate enough. I even find myself thinking about that as I kiss him, making a considered effort to make it a real kiss, not a half-hearted, off-to-work kiss. I try to find something in us that used to be there. He says I am distant.

As soon as he tells me this, I become distant.

Once, many months ago, when it was sunny and exciting and still the season of light, the spring of hope, and all that, Charles also told me I was being distant. But then, it was a conscious effort on my part at cold turkey. I won't pretend it was easy, but it began on the day of a funeral—a real funeral, not my fantasy gothic melodrama—so Isobel was home too. It was also the day our polytunnels arrived, and his was being erected—even in this, it was him first. It was a beautiful, hot, summery April morning, and I was painting a fence. Charles was nearly helping a little bit, mostly by pointing out bits I missed, and trying not to get paint on his funeral suit. He was also overseeing the building of the tunnel, thinking of the funeral and staying busy by juggling Isobel on the porch and me in the yard.

Despite the heat, I was making progress. I stopped to make tea. Charles was sitting on his porch, like Mister Colonial, looking across his domain, while I was working in the sun, and the men constructing the tunnel were wilting. I really needed that cup of tea. And, as timing and circumstance would have it, that was also the time Charles decided to made coffee. He then sat with his coffee and his wife on the porch while I brought my own cup of tea from our office, across the yard, and painted while I drank.

I was missing being kissed, and having his company, divided or not. Any company that day would have sufficed, but today, I was the hired help, while he sat on the porch, looking down on his workers.

He came over. At last, he came over to me. But we were in full view of them all, so he just said to come for coffee. Of course, I would not. I had just made my own tea, and now I was sulking, because he had left it too late to think of me. So, I drank my tea and continued working, and they went to the funeral. By mid-afternoon, the polytunnel was up, and the painting was finished. I left early, to avoid being caught in the funeral traffic as it passed through the village. I drove past the little church on the hilltop, past the modern church farther along the road, and onwards to my daughter's school. I bumped up onto the curb outside the school and cut the engine. Having arrived ar too early, I sat in the car to wait and passed the time thinking about how I felt like the hired help. I tried not to mind, because I understood a funeral is a funeral, and had Isobel not been there, I would have surely still been kissed.

But then I thought maybe we were wrong, and if we could manage a day without kissing each other, we could manage for longer. If we could manage for longer, we could put this thing in its box and nail down the lid. I maintained this not kissing stance the next day, and the next, and maybe even the next, then he cornered me in their laundry room, and he told me I was distant.

I told him then that I was trying for cold turkey, but I didn't tell him I'd felt like the hired help. I told him I was not kissing him, and he was not kissing me, and we must continue not kissing each other, because we both had other people to kiss, and I tried to be firm about it. Then we looked at each other, and that was enough; it was too hard to not kiss, and far too easy to do so. So, we kissed. And we kissed, and we kissed. The world immediately resettled on its axis, and everything felt right again after the days of missing his touch. It always felt so right. Even now, even this far on, even when I am 'not allowed' to contact him or communicate, I know, in his arms, I would feel so very right.

That was my only attempt to put this thing we had going on back into its box, and I gave in so easily to letting it stay out of the box. James doesn't realise that when he accuses me of 'being distant' today, he rejuvenates a flood of memory, and I recall that moment in the laundry room. Inevitably, I become not only distant, but far away in the thrill of fourteen months ago when I was exactly where I wanted to be: entwined in Charles's arms, kissing him in the laundry room, while the linen tumbled and tangled in the drier behind us.

I am afraid there will always be something that takes me back there—a memory, a song, a misplaced word—and I will never be able to let it go completely. I'm afraid of the memories, and yet, I cherish them too; I don't want to let go of that most magical time in my life. It was the Season of Light and the Spring of Hope—and the hottest, brightest spring for years.

CHAPTER TEN

BROKEN WINGS

I don't know enough. There is so much I should learn still, if only I had the time and the patience. I will have the time, for I have nothing else to do now, but I won't have enough time quickly enough. I want to go to market in two weekends' time, and I don't know how to glaze my pieces. I know glazes are dangerous if misused, but I don't know how to use them properly. I don't have time to learn, so I apply them regardless. Today I have painted glaze onto one set of Snakes and Ladders tiles, but my intention to paint carefully is hindered by my laziness in using a brush too big for the job at hand, and I smudge the edges. I could wash off the mistakes and begin again. Instead, I try to cover my mess by painting, uncarefully, over it all instead, then I rub off the excess. This is not helping things improve. It just looks like sloppy work and something I didn't care about very much. I rub off more and more of the paint and am left with what I now think is a rather nice vintage effect that will either work out all right or not really work out at all. Not for the first time I question the sense of trying to pay the bills with something I don't know how to do, but what else can I try instead? I am not really sure of anything anymore, so I decide to leave my unfinished work on my increasing pile of 'things to deal with later'.

James thinks I should be less frugal with the electricity for firing the kiln and fire it tomorrow with the pieces I have ready. He is, of course, probably right. My justification is as warped as always; I have the optimism that all my pieces will turn out fine to buffer me from worrying that they may not. I cannot waste kiln space and the electricity in firing a half-load if it all works, but it will be such a huge waste of time and clay and energy and resources if I fill the kiln and everything cracks or falls apart during the firing.

I've broken the wings of three out of thirteen angels. Is an angel still an angel if it has no wings? Two have been filed down into fairies instead, and one is entirely without wings, but now she reminds me of Anna, who has been a true angel to me for these last months, these months that feel as long as forever—an angel without wings, looking out for me always. The angel on my shoulder is grateful that ten of thirteen are still good, so I am still winning. There are cracks in the glaze of their hair; so many more may become fallen angels yet. I hope any that don't fire well will be salvageable by covering with acrylic paint. That was always plan A anyway, for at least I have painted before. Plan B dictated that I should try out the glaze, for a less amateur finish. James said I should glaze; he agrees that glaze would make my pieces seem less handmade.

I don't want any of these pieces to look homemade, but to look 'I can't believe you made that' professional, so I need the glazing to work. But I know so little, and I may not know enough, so they may become increasingly amateur as time goes by. I need them to look amazing so people will come to my stall at market and be amazed, impressed, and astounded.

They will flatter me and compliment me, and I will feel I'm doing okay and that I'll come through this still. I don't want to be passed by, even by the strangers who I hope will become my customers. I don't want to fail again and feel I must find a real job and fill my days with the tedium of answering to someone else's life. I don't want to work for someone else when, for the past four years, I had that stimulating combination of work and play that Charles and I had created. I know now I am selfish enough to want to do only what I *want* to do. However, I must pay the bills from the decisions I make, so I must make them work, or I will have no choice but to find a real job.

I wonder, again, if Charles ever considers that I now have no job, no income, no work. I wonder if he thinks of me at all. I wonder if the label I have so easily given him of 'Spineless' is real or if he is, in fact, the stronger one of the two of us still. Now, on this cold, dark Monday evening, I am parked outside his house while our children have their French lesson. I leave the engine running to keep myself warm, and I fill that cold, lonely thirty minutes by contemplating how much strength it takes him to pretend I am not there. I am curious about what story he has given to his children to explain why I can no longer sit inside with my feet propped on his range, tea in my hand, stretching a half-hour lesson into two hours of nothing and everything. I wonder what reason he has given to explain why my daughter can no longer go into the house after class to play until, when we can no longer put it off, I drag her home to bed. I wonder too, how long we can sustain this pretence as the weather becomes colder and the evenings darker. Today, his youngest daughter stands on the doorstep, asking questions. Charles's oldest daughter comes to help, puts an arm around her youngest sister, and pulls her close.

"She doesn't need to talk to him today," she says gently reaching her other hand towards my own daughter and holding her close.

I do. I do need to talk to him. I do. I try to hide my tears as I lean against my car, talking to these children who I love so much, but Charles's oldest daughter is crying too.

He doesn't need to talk to me. That is what she really means. But then, how will I know how he is? I can't ask her, and I can't see him, but I know he is not all right at all. I know, too, I am not who he wants to tell anything to anymore. How does Isobel think that stops me from caring? My closest friend is hurting and shutting himself away. He is pretending I am not sitting in my car outside his house in the cold and the dark. I am hurting too, and he knows that about me, just exactly like I know it about him. If he had truly forgotten it all, he would have no need to hide. He can only force himself to forget while he still remembers. And I must force myself to keep my distance.

With nowhere else to go anymore, I go home and paint my angels, and when they are broken, I try to turn the pieces into something new that will not be quite the same or quite the way I planned it to be. I cannot control it all, and I must make the best of what I have left, for to throw it all away is to waste everything I have learned.

CHAPTER ELEVEN

ABANDONED

*T*he kiln is on, and I am desolate. Motivation has run out, and I can't work on anything new today. Instead of walking Jess on the shortest possible main road route and disappearing up the bog lane, I laugh in the face of danger and stay on the road—and at a time I know Isobel may be passing through, no less. I feel as if I know her routine better than I know my own. (Her days will still be the same: get up, drive past my house to take her children to school, go to her work at the community hospital, home for lunch—that's new; she didn't used to come home, but now she needs to check that Charles is where she left him, I guess —then she'll return to work, stay late on Wednesdays, finish early on Fridays, same old, same old. I don't have much of a routine now. I get up. I take my son to meet his bus. I take my daughter to school. At some point later, I collect her. I meet his bus. The other bits blur.) I feel let down that, on the day I am ready for her to mow me down, she does not pass, and I am still standing. I wave to Charles's brother as he passes, but no further relief comes from walking today. It seems odd that so many times in my old life, I passed her or she passed me, whenever or wherever we might be driving, but now when I wish her to be here, she is not. Instead of being run down, Jess and I lean on a fence and gaze at the mountains, and I notice I am not yet fully insane. Today I am glad it's a damp and dreary October day, for, had the day been bright and dry, sunny and warm, I know I would sink onto the grass verge and stop.

Really stop.

Today I feel I have done *enough,* and I am exhausted from still being here. If it were dry and sunny, I would surrender to the darkness in my mind and sit at the roadside, alone with my dog. Instead, the last remaining fragments of my sanity remind me that the grass is wet, and so will my butt be if I sit on the damp ground. The dregs of my rationale convince me that I would, eventually, be dragged home by hunger and necessity, so I may as well stay standing, and go home with a dry bum.

The news reports more job cuts today. A big insurance firm is dropping hundreds of jobs, with notice, and severance pay. Where is the news bulletin for me? I have lost my job, with no notice, and no severance pay. I am wondering whether Charles is struggling to pay his mortgage and feed his children. I wonder whether he has even noticed that in any other job, I would have at least a leg to stand on. To be a partner in an unequal partnership means one partner can choose to force the other to tell their children there is no food today. I wonder what kind of friend can do this and how his conscience is still staying quiet. Then I realise it is the same kind of person who could tell me his wife is his best friend and he loves her, while he holds me in his arms and kisses me. Then I realise I am also that person, just the same as he is, and the blame is mine too. But it is hard to share even the blame with someone who has forgotten how to share.

Only a few short weeks ago, at the beginning of September, when we still had dreams and hope and plans, and thought the business still had a future, we made a phoenix for an event where we would be showcasing our business. The phoenix would symbolize the work we had done to rebuild his farm from a dying business into an exciting, viable venture. It would soar, bright and eye-catching, strung from wires, above our marquee. I'd created him from an idea Charles had, and the phoenix rose as an epitome of our level of understanding of each other. This time, it was Charles who spoke an idea out loud, and I who translated his idea into a solid, 3-D, chicken wire and coloured-latex reality. So many other times, it had been me who had voiced an idea, and Charles who had turned my thoughts and dreams into a solid and tangible creation. We had made this phoenix together, only a few short weeks before the bottom fell out of our world. That phoenix we had made in the summer was to signify there was still hope.

Even then, I was still desperately clinging onto the idea of hope, when really none was left at all.

Even then, Charles was happy to pretend everything was fine.

Now I must make a new phoenix for myself, and I am itching to make a felted phoenix, with the bag of wool I salvaged from the ruins of the art workshops we wrote so many articles about and discussed so often on our media channels. I can see this new phoenix in my mind, but he must wait, for he will take too long to make, and I won't be able to pay the bills with him. I have settled, instead, for drawing him in clay, on a set of tiles I have titled *The Bog Fire*. These tiles are not dry enough to put in the kiln today, so they make the beginning of a new load. It is good I have the start of a new load, for I haven't made enough yet to take to market, and I know, I know my list is still too long for the time I have. I should even now be rolling out slabs of clay and cutting the next batch. It is an added benefit of working with clay that I cannot stop for too long or the work-in-progress will dry out and spoil before I can finish it. I must keep going, every day, to make this work. It gives me something I must get up for every morning. I can do this. I can be strong. I will be a phoenix. I can be a phoenix. I am a phoenix.

But my feet are wet from standing on the verge gazing at the mountains, and my fire is out. I will be a phoenix tomorrow instead.

CHAPTER TWELVE

DANGER

*I*t is a dark and stormy night. I have negotiated flood warnings and fallen branches just to leave my own driveway. Funny how this short journey to Charles's home now feels like the longest and most dangerous journey I make these days. But, here I am again; having survived last week's French lesson, once again, I find myself sitting in the car outside Charles's house, in the dark, in the rain, with only Charles's cold, wet dog coming out to talk to me. I tell myself I am continuing these lessons for my daughter and for Charles's youngest daughter, and that is true, as they are as close as siblings and need to see each other. However, it cannot be the whole truth, for if it were only for them, it wouldn't be such an ordeal in my head, and I wouldn't shake like a leaf before and after, and while I sit here in the car.

That only the dog will offer company is not strictly true. Although I suspect the company of Charles is not freely or willingly given, he does, nonetheless, come out at my request that I need to talk to him for a minute, and we engage in a civil conversation. We pass needless remarks about the weather, and we talk briefly of accounts and accountants. I can't make eye contact, for fear of what he would see in me, so I can't know how he really is, except he has lost weight. He is not the man he used to be.

As we talk, we put on an act that we know each other well enough to see through; we pretend, as we have been instructed, that we do not know each other at all. We can make no eye contact, for if we do, we would understand everything we have been through during the past few weeks. We would see into each other's hearts, and I would know if he is coping or if he is hurting too. I do understand he doesn't want to let me know how he is feeling; and that he does not want to see I am not okay. If we don't look at each other, we can pretend we are both fine, even while we know we are not. I have longed all week to see him, but now . . . now, of course, it isn't enough. It will never be enough again. I am out here in the rain in the dark in the car, waiting for the lesson to end, and he is back inside, pretending I am not here at all.

As time drags into the last days of October, it is another dark and stormy night, after another dark and stormy day, but I have *made progress.* I have moved my clay from the kitchen table to my new studio space—just a tidied-up garden shed, but it feels like progress nonetheless—and I have diligently worked through the day. There are finally kings to add to the nativity set—as always, in history and in story books, they arrived after everyone else, but here they are now, bearing gifts and wonky crowns. I am pleased with them so far, regardless of their wonkiness, and tomorrow they will be dry enough for re-shaping and finishing. I have started to gloss-glaze some of last week's pieces, but, once again, I don't know enough. Poor Joseph, first glazed and bewildered by the birth of a child that wasn't his, is now thickly and clumsily glazed by me. I wonder if I can wash him off and start again.

It is telling how, even in that very earliest of stories of infidelity, Joseph, like James, remained dignified and solid—supporting, loving, and most definitely on the highest of all the moral high grounds. I wonder what happened behind their own closed doors, in that little, flat-roofed house in Nazareth. I wonder if it is blasphemy to wonder that. Surely, even Joseph had what James insists on calling his 'wobbles'. Surely Joseph considered walking away and not returning. Surely, he at least briefly considered at what speed his donkey must gallop into the nearest palm tree to end it all, bereft as he must have been with the knowledge of Mary carrying a child that Joseph hadn't created. Did he lie awake at night, speculating about punching his rival's nose? Did he find out whether jealously, anger, rage, and love would mean even a gentle man could throw the hardest punch? And yet, they—Mary and Joseph—according to public image, came through it all as a happy family, with a happy ever after, and became parents to the son who was supposed to have saved the world from pain and suffering. James, like Joseph, offers his errant wife support, practical advice, and is always the parent our children need while their mother is too bewildered to cope.

It surprised, touched, and then overwhelmed me that Charles's oldest daughter was pleased to see me last week. After Charles had gone inside, she came out to talk. I got out of the car and stood under cover of their porch as my daughter and Charles's youngest spilled from the office and came chattering across the yard to find us. The youngest daughter threw herself at me, and as I hugged her back before gently untangling her and pushing her away, the older girl stepped in to hug me too. It has, of course, got me into

Isobel's latest drunken text rant, but, at the time, it was a glimmer of gold in a grey October. I hadn't considered any possibility other than anger or resentment from the older children. I hadn't considered that I, too, might be missed as much I am missing. I was pleased and saddened to be the recipient of that unexpected hug. I was filled with an unexpected gladness at the reassurance from her that it is not my fault. I presume that means the children have, so far, been protected from hearing, or overhearing, the sordid truth. How could I say, "But it is, it is my fault, at least in part," when it will never be my place to tell her this? Even at seventeen, our two oldest children must be protected from what we have done. Part of me is glad to allow a moment to consider that maybe she thinks all of this is her father's fault; perhaps she does know, but she understands I love him and that he has hurt us all. For the second week running, I try helplessly to stifle tears as I talk to this girl, and she cries too. How would there not be tears when I miss the children and the children miss me? How would there not be tears when our whole world has changed in a heartbeat? After this illicit conversation with the oldest child, a message from Isobel was inevitable; I know she will need to tell me not to talk to her children. My tears anger her, she does not understand them. Nonetheless, it still catches me unawares, almost an entire week later, when I am the recipient of the emotional outburst bleeping into my inbox to inform me that my own emotional outbursts are unwelcome.

Dear Isobel,

Thank you for your emotional outburst to ask me not to have any emotional outbursts. It is good of you, as always, to tell me not to reply, just in case we begin an everlasting text conversation reminding each other not to have emotional outbursts.

Among the many things I cannot comprehend, I cannot comprehend her lack of understanding that this is an emotional time for me, as well as for her. How can she not understand I have lost the family I've known for the last four years and that her family have lost me? How can she not understand that for me to leave everything I ever wanted behind me, with the tears I shed on her doorstep, will undoubtedly make me cry and cry and cry? I know I am the cheater and not the cheated, but, at times like this, it still feels as if we have lost the same things, Isobel and me. I can still put myself in her shoes, so why can she no longer fit into mine? Her text is emotional, with misspellings and anger, and I can tell she has been drinking.

Dear Isobel,

You should hide your phone before you open wine.

There is an element of hypocrisy I must admit to, as I send this text with the uncomfortable knowledge that I, too, should hide my own wine, along with my phone.

Dear Isobel,

It is good of you to keep up this regular contact, approximately once weekly, I believe so far, to remind me not to have any contact with you. I appreciate it.

She clearly doesn't realise I will think of her weekly even without her reminding me not to think of her. Daily, even. Hourly, in fact. I wonder will there ever come a time when she and Charles do not fill my thoughts in all my waking hours?

Dear Isobel,

Why don't you realise that each time you contact me, it triggers a thousand memories, and I then spend far longer thinking of your husband than I was before your message came through?

Although I was pleased to have seen him, and to have

spoken to him, while the girls had their lesson on that dark night, and to have remained calm and civil, I then go to bed thinking of him, and wishing it was not like this. I lie against my own husband—I drape my arms and legs around and across and over him—but it is not him I am thinking of as I fall asleep.

Dear Isobel,

Which of us is Charles thinking of as he lies next to you and falls asleep?

CHAPTER THIRTEEN

ONE OF MANY BEGINNINGS

*I*t is still raining. There are floods across Ireland; shopping centres are underwater, rivers have burst, and people have been swept away. The water has nowhere left to go, yet more and more falls. My garden is sodden, and so am I. I am relieved, despite everything, we are no longer planning for our autumn events, and that, at least, is something to be grateful for.

For me, the first defining moment of the shift in our relationship came in the autumn of two years ago. We had been working together for around eight months by then and were comfortable in each other's company. We had quickly become like children around each other: tentative at first as we worked each other out, then thrown together to play without inhibitions or boundaries. We knew each other well already and enjoyed our days together. I no longer knocked at the door before entering his home, and he made my tea how he knew I liked it. After a first couple of months of finding our feet in the new business, we were already working together in harmony. Very quickly, we realised we could communicate effectively across the heads of staff and visitors, with messages conveyed with a single meeting of the eyes. I thought nothing of taking his cup of tea from his hands, taking a sip, and passing it back for him to continue drinking. Already, we shared intimacies I did not freely share with others. As we grew more confident in each other's company, our childlike fun settled and developed into something more akin to a teenage crush: that first Halloween brought with it the first hug, and the beginning of many more.

It had rained and rained and rained, like it is now, but we'd had to work through the weather to get things ready. The full quota of guests had booked into the forest chalets for the half-term break, and I had so many articles to write, photos to take, diaries to present. He still needed to cut and light a new path to make the newest cabin more easily accessible, and I followed him around like a puppy, camera at the ready to record his every move. At times, as always, I would hang the camera from a handy branch and muck in, hacking at branches, hammering hand-painted signposts, and making suggestions and changes as we worked in harmony together.

That week, Charles was distracted by houseguests. I was working in the forest, ensuring I had the right lighting and set up for filming at night, and James was with me. Whilst Charles remained in his house, James was putting his own electrical skills to task by systematically checking and installing lighting along the forest paths for guests to negotiate the forest safely, even in the dark. Our children played in the house with Charles's children, and I didn't allow myself to think about how much time I no longer spent with them, because I knew they were happy and loved inside the farmhouse with their newfound 'extra family'. We had also organised a Halloween event for families, where they would take a spooky walk through the trees, then be warmed with pumpkin soup and gentle frights. It was another string to our ever-extending bow, and the event was already sold out. Together, James and I worked through the rain, and into the dark, night after night, and Charles was inside making dinner for his friends. I was raging.

James had taken time off his own paid work to install lighting for our fledging business, and I ineffectively did what I could to help him. In truth, my help is no use when I am raging, so after I'd checked my own necessities for filming, I left James to work on alone, while I sulked in the office and Charles went shopping to buy food to feed his houseguests.

As the time we needed the paths to be ready closed in, I oversaw the preparation of the chalets and made new signs for the new path. I answered the phone and took more bookings. James installed more lighting. And Charles drank coffee with his guests.

It went on like this for the week before the mid-term break, so I was boiling over with anger that I was doing all the work in what was meant to be a partnership. I was even doing the work that was not in my skillset or prearranged remit; I was a photographer and journalist, above all, not a handyman or lumberjack. I was disgusted with Charles that James—James who had a job of his own—was here working for us, while Charles was not. In the only letter Charles ever wrote to me, he apologised half-heartedly for his over-stretching and having guests to deal with. He proposed that, if I believed he was not pulling his weight, we could have a serious review after the chalet guests had left, after the Halloween event, once the mid-term was over. I agreed, and he agreed to help James finish, and then, later that evening, he made dinner for his guests, while James and I worked on. James and my children went in to join them for dinner, and I went home, and, for the first time, I accidentally sent James a text I had meant for Charles and sent Charles the one I had meant for James. In slightly different words to each of them, I told them both they should eat without me, for I was still raging.

Their replies were almost identical—James urging me to swallow my annoyance, reminding me that I needed to eat, so come and eat. The reply from Charles said more concisely, **_Please come and eat with us._** In these few words, I knew he knew I was upset, and his _Please_ was shorthand for the apology he knew he needed to issue. Pride and hurt sent me home anyway, alone and upset, while James and our children ate dinner in the midst of the family I wanted to belong to.

Before the first people arrived for the Halloween week of forest-living, and before the crowds arrived for the evening events, I cornered Charles to tell him I needed to talk my anger through. He followed me into the office, where I stood with my back to him, pretending to be busy with filling the booking lists while I gathered my thoughts. With shaking hands, I dropped the book back onto the table and clenched my hands instead. I wiped my eyes with the back of my sleeve, trying not to let the tears spill over. This was the first time I had cried in front of him. He responded to my tears by asking if he could give me a hug. I moved without thinking, straight into his outstretched arms, and it felt like I was finally in the place I knew I was supposed to be.

After all our visitors had checked out, and Charles and I had tidied away the remnants of their stay, I was still angry with how he had behaved before. Now that we finally had time to talk, we talked and talked. He heard my anger, and he listened to my complaints. He told me I was good for him, and I never, ever, got to ask him why or in what way, or even to ask him *how* I was good for him. As I got in my car to leave that day, he looked at me as if I was everything to him, and that was the moment I knew for certain I was not the only one feeling more than friendship between us. Since that moment, I cannot forget how he told me I was good for him, and how he looked at me as if I were his whole world. I do not believe a look like that can be a lie.

CHAPTER FOURTEEN

LOST MARBLES

*H*ow strange it is that when I tell new people—strangers I have only just met—that I was running my own business until my partner pulled out suddenly, that they assume it is my husband who has left me. I wonder if it's the way I tell it or the use of the word *'partner'*, or that something in me gives away that my heart is aching.

I have entered a new stage of my life, and it brings something I never expected either to become or to enjoy. I'm now officially a market trader. And I like it. I stand behind a table laden with my wares, unable to go very far or do anything very much. My first Saturday at market went like this:

I got some tea. I talked to some fellow traders who came to chat. I made small talk with a few browsers. I got some tea. I sewed some bags for my juggling balls, using recycled pieces of cut-up blankets. I talked to some customers. I got some tea. I felt calm and relaxed and comfortable and as if there really was nowhere else to worry about. Best of all, I even sold enough to cover the €25 cost of the stall. What a buzz! People actually liked the things I made and said so many lovely things!

Perhaps this will work out for me and things will get better from here. I go back again on Sunday, and I will go every weekend until Christmas.

My pitch is near to the café and the stairs. It is the first or the last stall as shoppers enter the café or use the stairs. I suppose it is only reasonable I should be the stallholder to be informed that, "There's a dead mouse on the staircase." I'm proud of the new couldn't-care-too-much-about-other-people self I'm working on, and I simply tell the poor woman who discovers the mouse that it's my first time here, and I don't know who should be told. I don't leap to my feet and shout helpfully, "Don't worry. I'll deal with it." I don't move the mouse, and I don't care. I don't even feel guilty, and I don't think about it again until much later when my daughter's friend arrives with her parents, and I send the girl to see what has now become the dramatic and therefore capitalised Dead Mouse on the Staircase. It's become an adventure, rather than something I feel guilty about for not dealing with. In my previous life, I would never have relaxed in the knowledge that I knew about the Dead Mouse on the Staircase, yet did nothing.

I also realised today that, in this new environment, I can be somebody else. I can be somebody new, somebody different. I can concoct a new story. If people believe my story is that my husband is the one who left me, then I can let them. It is ironic that James is the husband who *hasn't* left me, and that the husband who has left me was not my own to start with.

Someone on a stall near mine sells pretty beads and shiny things. It reminds me of the new game I have installed on my phone, which I pull out to play on while there is a lull in the customers milling around the market. It's just another distraction to help me procrastinate—another delay tactic in the great scheme of *Getting on With My Life*, another waste of time, to stop me from thinking of the ways I used to spend my time and the ways in which I want to spend my time. It involves dropping virtual marbles in a virtual jar, to make all the marbles that are the same disappear. When the jar is empty, I have won. I realise suddenly that, even with marbles, I can't focus on the one in the present, but I'm forever looking at the one coming next. This leads to mistakes, and the marbles fall where I did not want them to land. Is this what it is to be me? That the thing that might happen next will distract from the thing already in front of me? I change up a level to 'difficult' today, and realise it is just as my life was. There are suddenly even more pretty things to deal with—the marbles are in more colours, more patterns—and there is suddenly no room in the jar to fit them, although I think I want them all. I must sacrifice some to make room for others, and sometimes even the prettiest ones must be dropped. These fall outside of the jar, and I don't even notice when they don't go away but lie there patiently waiting for me to pay them some attention. James is a marble I dropped outside the jar. Charles is all the pretty ones I tried to keep. Charles is all the marbles I want to play with and hold in my hands and run through my fingers. James is the marble waiting for me, patiently, outside the jar until I notice he is there.

Even now, after all that has happened, I still want Charles to be a pretty marble I can keep.

I should switch back to 'easy' and pretend the pretty marbles were never there. Charles seems to have done exactly that, and very effectively. How will I know if he ever remembers I was even in his life? How can he not remember, when I cannot forget? For four years, I had conversation with him every day, and I am so lonely without it.

In the market on Sunday, I see a woman I think is Isobel. She is across the room, browsing in a different aisle. She walks away from me, towards the vegetable stall in the far corner. In my runaway mind, she turns towards me, rushes at me, tips my table, scatters my clay, breaks my pieces. She destroys my work, again. Even when I realise it is not her, I see her again and again through the afternoon. Although she is never Isobel, each time I catch a glimpse of her, my heart leaps with fear, but also with hope, that this time it will be her. I am protective of my ceramic pieces, but even more so of my new friends and fellow traders. They think I am strong and that my husband has left me. They do not know another man's wife could ruin everything I have made if she came across my stall at the market, and that I have destroyed everything she had.

Charles's brother came in yesterday. We discussed the weather and nothing, but when he had left, I watched for him to return. I hoped to see him again. I wanted him to have shaken off his own wife and children, and then, only then, I might have been able to ask what I really wanted to ask him; "How is Charles?" I think he would have known what I meant and understood all the many questions I would have been asking in that one question. I don't think he would have answered any of them properly; he would have just told me everything is fine, just fine. I didn't see him again, so I didn't get to ask him my one burning question, and he didn't have to answer or not answer it. I wonder if he will mention to Charles that he saw me.

It feels strange be a market trader, selling the things I have created on the foundations of my broken heart and some leftover dreams. I have already given my heart, soul, and indeed my body, to Charles, but having lost my job to our mistakes as well, I must now give away even more of myself. I feel as if I am selling my life, in the hope of paying my bills and feeding my children.

But, surprisingly, I like it. I like it here in the market, and I will go again. The other stallholders are friendly and include me easily in their banter. Sometimes they offer to get me tea; they pass the time with conversation about nothing, and I can be someone else here. It feels a little bit like finding a new home.

I am both delighted and sad to sell the tile set with the *Bog Fire* painting. The buyer will never fully understand what that picture signifies. It is the burning and the burnt; the dead and the flames; the devastation, and above all, the phoenix—always the phoenix. It is the picture I did for Charles and for everything we burned. It is for rising from ashes, but also for wanting to rise with him. My customer liked it, but she wasn't sure. She liked the other set too, but one of those was warped, and that was enough to settle her choice. What she will never know is the set she didn't buy was about love and brightness, hope and dreams—and that the set with the fire and the phoenix is more warped than the other one could ever be. She can't know the pictures with the phoenix and the fire are about love and destruction and the burning pain a person is left with when their world ends.

It is strange to feel at home so soon in a new space, with new people, and to be able to reinvent and start again, and yet . . . and yet they *'get me'* already. I have explained I am there on the strength or weaknesses of my failed business and a month (only a month) of thumping clay. They, too, acknowledge the irony of thumping clay in sadness, anger, and frustrated tears, and making angels from that. They see it as "Hope" and "A Sign" and "Strength." I see only "Irony" and "Mercenary" and "Desperation." I am cheating once more by selling people angels I don't believe in. Nevertheless, and whatever the reason, I will make more angels, as people seem to need them.

CHAPTER FIFTEEN

TO MAKE MY OWN CHOICE

*W*hen I was a child, my brothers had these books called, *Choose Your Own Adventure.* Maybe that is exactly what I need now:

"Turn to page 56 for a happy ending."

"Turn to page 72 if I am so very in the wrong that I deserve to die a slow and painful death at the hands of Isobel's revenge."

"Turn to page 407 if Isobel is as deluded as me."

And that sort of thing. I want a happy ending, but I don't know what a happy ending will be. The happiness I want will always mean someone else is unhappy. But if they are happy, then I am not. I must be a truly evil person that my happiness depends on another person's unhappiness. But what, really, is happiness?

I struggle to see that happiness can come from clinging onto a dead relationship, or one that has lost its fire. Even comfortable, old slippers eventually fall apart and must be discarded. In a lucky life, they will be put in a clothing bank and recycled to bring someone else warm feet or a plate of food or a well for clean water. In the worst-case scenario, they are so worn out that they are nothing but landfill. I think it must be better to throw something away while it can be good for someone else. Surely, we should minimize landfills wherever we can, and if the people who are no longer loved as much or in the same passionate way as they once were can be recycled into someone else's *Everything,* then that must be a happier ending? I do not wish either James or Isobel to be nothing but landfill. Especially not James, who is a wonderful father to our children and is comfortable and familiar. I love him, but is it fair to try to pretend I have the passion he needs from me?

If I hadn't noticed that I can still find that passion, albeit somewhere else, perhaps it would be of no matter, and I would resign myself to the life we have. But the glimpse of another page, another chapter, another story, wants me to say, *"Turn to page 345, and they are all happy."* I think that on this other page, they will be happy with people other than those they are with now. I wonder though if the individual pages of happiness count at all if the ending is not a happy one?

I want to believe in love, but even that is too complicated, for if I believe in love, and those countless clichés about love conquering all, then we should be in love with the ones who are in love with us. If James loves me with the same passion I have for Charles, and Charles has remembered he might still have that love for Isobel, and her passion is directed only at hating me, then how can love ever conquer *anything?* I want to believe Charles loves me in some way, but he wants to believe he doesn't. He wants to believe now that I am no one —not the woman whose life he turned upside down by a look that said he loved me and a kiss "because he wanted to."

I avoided that kiss for so very long. We shared so many hugs and touches and looks and understandings since that first hug in the October aftermath of our Halloween fight. We soaked up endless warmth, comfort, love from just being near each other. We had the undeniable knowledge of the crash course we were on, but still, I kept my head down always. For months, or weeks, or infinite cloudy mists of time, I kept my head down, comfortable in his arms but afraid to look up for the danger of the inevitable and the unstoppable. I ask myself over and over what changed on that day when he said, "Come here," just as I was about to leave, and, trusting him completely, without question, I came to him. And looked up.

I only remember the clarity of a clash of teeth, an apology after, and my own reassurance not to be sorry and my own suggestion that maybe sometime we would do it again. And so, we did. Again and again and again; too much and never enough. I long to be there again, comfortable in his arms, again and again and again, too much, but never enough. Return to the beginning and don't turn the pages that make it end. I am honest with myself enough to know that if this were truly a *Choose Your Own Adventure,* I would choose to be stuck in that first chapter forever, reading the same paragraph over and over.

I knew for months that my story would bring me to the point of being in his arms, but I never saw that it would bring me here afterwards. Now, someone else—he and his wife— have torn my book from my hands and ripped out my pages. They have closed the book and changed the order. My story is no longer mine, and someone else is turning my pages. I have the memories, but if he now chooses to dis-remember the story, how can I tell if I remember it right? So many of our fights were centred around my rememberings being different to his, and my sense of my own sanity fell into question and disarray. I know, in reality, he remembers more than he wants to. I know that, too, is why he cannot talk to me anymore, but why he could still wake me by watching me sleep one night in a shared tent on a working weekend in August, well over a year after our affair had ended.

When I am kind to myself, I believe his decision to end the business was initiated by his terrified knowledge that he still remembered too much—feelings as well as memories. I think, when I am kind to myself, it became too hard for him to fight it and easier for him to let me go. When I am not kind to myself but simply heartbroken, sad, lonely, and aching with the pain of loss, I believe he hates me and blames me for ruining his life. I think it came from him needing to end it before Isobel did. He knew, when he told Isobel what we had done, there would be no other choice but for her to demand the end of the business. I think he needed to be able to tell her he had already severed our partnership, drawn the line, put himself firmly back on her side. Whatever the story, I can't believe he doesn't remember what I remember. How will I ever know my own story if he has stolen my plot?

It occurs to me that none of us would choose to have the same happy ending I would choose, and the one I would choose is not the one I should want either. Charles and James and Isobel would all choose the ending where I fall back in love with my own husband and live happily ever after, but some things cannot be put back in their box once they have been let out, and this, I worry, is one of them. I have become expanding foam, and I am no longer the size or shape to fit into James's life. I wish I could honestly say I hope Charles is more successful with putting himself back into his own box, but, in all truth, I don't want him to, nor do I understand how he can. It will spring out on him one day, like a Jack-in-the-Box with a faulty catch, for how can Isobel ever truly trust him now? I wonder if he feels like he got out of our frying pan only to jump straight into a fire and if he will spend the rest of his marriage trying to keep that fire under control. I wonder how long it will be before the flames take over completely and finish destroying the things we started to burn years ago.

And I wonder and I wonder and I wonder if thoughts of me still linger in the ashes of his dreams.

CHAPTER SIXTEEN

UNFRIENDLY

I hear the word *"tenacity"* on the radio and love it enough to need to use it. I am keeping a tenacious grip on the shadow of our friendship. Charles, however, is not.

I am not the only one experiencing drama and heartache. My dear friend Anna has also recently come out of a relationship with an *unsuitable* man. He was married, but at least he'd had the decency to separate from his wife before starting a relationship with Anna. As it turned out, this didn't make it much easier; he still has too much baggage, too many commitments, too much selfishness to share Anna with his old life. She is missing her man too, so she empathizes with me missing mine. (Neither of us should really lay claim to ownership of these men; the use of the word *'mine'*, whilst hopeful, is an untrue description. We use it from want and longing, not from any truth.) I can understand everything she feels, as fundamentally, we have both lost people we loved. It relieves me that despite her own heartache, she still gives time to mine.

They are ahead of Charles and me, in the falling apart of

their togetherness, but she, too, longs for contact and needs to exert her own willpower to not send random texts into the night, spurred onwards by yearning and loneliness. Her difference is that her man also has lapses of willpower. He is as likely to contact her "by mistake" as she is him. Today, she's found an old text from this man, from way back at the end of the summer when my own drama was beginning to unravel. She hadn't even opened it. I am amazed and disbelieving that she wouldn't have noticed when it came through—I would never miss a text from Charles; I notice *all* the texts that Charles does *not* send me, never mind any that he does, in fact, send. I notice the silence, and I miss the sound my phone used to make.

Anna and I quickly became wary of texting each other, as every time our phones bleep, we receive a physical jolt and an instant of hope in case it is the person we really want it to be. It never is. So, I do not text Anna anymore, because every message I send her now has to begin with an apology that I am not the man she wants to hear from, and because every time her phone buzzes to announce a new text, her heart will skip a beat with hope and fear and longing. I know this is true because she is a reflection of me.

Anna has tossed and turned in her mind the dilemma of what to say in belated answer—her decision to answer at all clearly already made—and eventually goes with friendly, polite, and enquiring, as to his well-being. She aimed for some nonchalance; he needed to hear his initial message had not been important enough in her life for her to answer it for a few months. I wonder if he will guess that she simply didn't answer because she didn't see his message but that, since discovering it two days ago, she has agonized and wondered and cried over it. I wonder if he will guess that her longing to hear from him, without knowing he had in fact contacted her, has been burning a hole through her heart?

I feel as if my own phone burns a hole in my heart and my pocket every time it rings, yet the times it shows Charles's number, I am scared to answer it. It *was* his number that showed on my screen over the weekend. I nearly couldn't answer; my hands shook, and my fingers and legs turned jellylike in those indecisive seconds before pressing 'accept'. It wasn't even him; his oldest daughter was calling to tell me that week's French lesson was cancelled. I wonder if this is the end of the lessons for my daughter.

We both have itchy fingers—Anna and I. We know we should not say all the things we want to say to the men who have thrown us from their lives, yet we cannot stop ourselves from firing out our thoughts in texts. We know they no longer want to hear these streams of consciousness. We know they don't want emotion and reminders. We know they do not care for out tears. Worse even than sending the texts, are the moments after. Will they reply? Will we instantly regret having sent them? Will we wish we had said more, less, or nothing at all? On days like this, I miss the Charles who was my dearest friend. I miss the cosy conversations, with my feet on his lap, and a mug of tea in my hands. I miss the comfort of our companionship and how he would be the person I could talk to about what was happening in Anna's life. On days like this, I really want to call him and say, "Hello, how are you?", or "What are you up to? I'm coming for tea." Instead, on days like this, I must walk Jess for miles and miles in futile efforts to stop the longing, so I don't send him that text and I don't call round for tea, despite how very much I want to.

Eventually my willpower fails me.

(It usually does.)

(I hate my lack of self-control.)

I texted Charles this evening, not to berate or complain or cry or reminisce but just to share news and irrelevant conversation like we always did. None of it meant anything except for the words I didn't include. "I miss you," "I'm still here," and "Do you think of me too?" I yearn for the conversation we used to share, every single day, for four years, and I hoped he heard what I said from the words I didn't use. *'Yearn',* like *'tenacious',* is another word I now fully understand the meaning of.

I don't expect a response, but I am so scared that he is determined to forget me, I feel I must remind him I am here to ensure he can't forget. I am not sure if everything I remember will still be real if I am the only one of us who remembers that it happened. If I can remember every touch, every look, every word, but he cannot or will not, is it only my own delusion that makes me think it was real?

This evening, he does respond, but not in the way I hoped. Despite being nearly forty and too old for this sort of thing, I'm checking Facebook, and he is gone from that part of my life too. I can't make myself understand how this man who was my friend, my business partner, my everything, and my last four years of life, can delete me with one click. I can't understand that Charles, who was everything—Charles, who kissed me "because he wanted to" and could look into my eyes as if I was meant for him—will no longer be my friend.

I can understand how he can no longer be my friend in all the same ways, but I can't understand how he can actively choose to click 'Remove' on my name. I, of course, have still learned nothing, and send a message. I know it is in response to my messages that he has unfriended me, yet I persist. I expect he will now block me from his Facebook, as Isobel has done already. Then I will no longer even show up in the osmosis generated by mutual Facebook friends, and he will be able to delete another part of me from his life. By blocking me, he will not even allow me to indulge in the pretence that he watches what I am doing with the fragments of my life. I have, of course, desperately, and with a huge side-serving of stupidity, instantly responded to his unfriending by sending him a friend request.

Be my friend; please be my friend again.

The rational part of my mind is disgusted by my desperation and neediness and keeps shouting at me.

"How is that a good idea?"

"Why would I want to be friends with a man like this after everything he has done and chosen to do?"

While that small, sane part of my mind tries to yell some sense at me, another part assures me that his withdrawal of friendship is not by his own choice but by Isobel's dictation. The rational side of my mind shouts louder that he is a grown man and will not be bulldozed by Isobel. The part of me that knows him so well allows that he will, in fact, be bulldozed by her. Completely. He is desperate to keep her.

I can't decide if he is stronger than me to allow her to block me from his life and his head and his heart, or if I am stronger. I, after all, can say to James, "Do not dictate who I can or cannot be friends with." I don't even need to say it aloud, for James knows it is not his place to dictate that.

I wish I could understand why it still matters so much to be friends with someone who can hurt me so much and treats me as if *everything* meant *nothing*. Why can he not remember who we were and what we gave each other? Why are there always so many whys, and why are none of them ever answered? Have I fallen so fast from being a grown up, to feeling like a teenager newly in love, to becoming nothing but a whining toddler? Why, why, why?

Is my tenacity just a pretty word I should replace with *'desperation'*, *'despair'*, *'desolation'*, and *'wretchedness'*? If I check in a thesaurus, will all those words be synonyms of *'tenacity'*? Does being tenacious just mean I have become an ego-centric bitch? A crazed stalker? Will my anger make me regret the things I have yet to say but will undoubtedly say soon? I am shocked to be so upset by being 'unfriended' in a virtual world, but it is the recognition I can be pushed from being 'ignored' to 'deleted' that hurts like a punch in the face. The crazy part of my head says, at least he was thinking of me as he did the unfriending. The rest of my mind refuses to listen, arguing that Charles's thinking of me in this instance counts for nothing at all. It is an unfriendly world when the people I loved and trusted the most can decide to 'unfriend' me for reasons we had built bridges over nearly eighteen months ago. We had promised ourselves that we could put the affair behind us, and continue as friends and business partners, and we had been doing this with reasonable success —businesswise, if nothing else—for the past eighteen months. If only I had accepted that as enough, not clung onto those remnants of hope, put my passions into the business and my own husband, if only … then maybe we would have not come to this heartache now. It is an unfriendly world when the man who promised that he, too, hoped we would come out of this as friends and let me believe he really meant that, has now pressed a 'Remove' button and deleted me from his life.

If this is who he really is, then who was the person I knew for four years?

CHAPTER SEVENTEEN

MISSING

 ear Charles,
    I wonder if you can help me. I am looking for someone I used to know, a long time ago, when my life was different. He has the same name as you, so I wonder if you know him, or remember knowing him at all? I used to be his business partner, and he was my closest friend. We shared everything, and we knew each other's hearts and minds. We complemented each other's skills and believed in each other's dreams. We believed in each other strongly enough to take our dreams and make them real, and we built a business that people loved. They loved us and the life we showed them. We took his land and my experience and my contacts and my knowledge of media and journalism, and we turned his farm into a lifestyle, and an adventure, a story, and paradise. He was kind and funny and strong and shared his life and his home and his soul with me.

In return, I gave him my ideas and my talents, my dreams and my time. Eventually, I even gave him my heart. Actually, to be honest, I gave him my heart quite quickly, for it didn't take long for me to think of him as a soulmate. We could read each other with a look and understand what we needed to tell each other without needing to speak aloud. We became closer and closer, both mentally and physically, and we played like children as we built our business. We grew like children too, then, began to act like teenagers in love. He kissed me eventually, and although I never made the first move, I may as well have had a neon flashing sign on my head stating I would be a willing recipient of his affections. I loved him as a friend, and then I loved him some more. I should never have been in love with him, and he should never have wanted to kiss me, for we were both married to other people. I would have given up everything for him, but although he mentioned it once or twice, he would never have given up his own everything for me. He wanted to have it all.

I thought by finding him, he had become my all.

He quickly realised he couldn't have everything, so he simply had sex with me before dumping me from the greatest height available and never looking back. For me, sex was the fullest sign of commitment I could offer. I was willing and available and yearning for him. For him, it was going out in his blaze of glory—having it all for one glorious moment before pulling my whole world out from under me. My bridges were burned, my marriage sacrificed, (although I hadn't yet got around to mentioning this to my husband, who must by now have sensed the cavern growing between us). (To be clear, we didn't actually have full sexual intercourse, but he seems to be a bit confused about this since the event and has rather madly told his wife we did.) (We did everything BUT that, you could remind him, although I would have done it, if he had not pushed me away at that final "we've gone too far.")

The Charles I used to know was the most generous person I ever knew, as well as the most selfish. Even after breaking my heart, we clung to our friendship, and I still had glimpses of the soulmate I used to know, whenever he forgot to pretend I was nothing anymore. Sometimes he did forget, then he would let me put my arms around him, or he'd put his around me. Sometimes he looked at me like he was thinking about kissing me again. I asked him once, and he said it was taking all his willpower to be 'just friends.' (He shouldn't have admitted that, as it gave me hope to cling to.) He stroked my hair and offered comfort when I cried over what we no longer had. But then he would remember he wasn't giving up his marriage and couldn't have it all. He would become cold and distant, and I would become emotional and angry, and would cry and rage. Eventually, my own husband demanded I tell him the whole story, then the Charles I used to know told his own wife too. After that, I never saw that same Charles again, although I thought I heard him once or twice in a split second on the phone, but only for a fleeting whisper before he went away again. I miss him every day, and I wonder if you know him, or where he is, or who he has become, for the person who you are is not the Charles I knew. If you ever see him again, tell him he was the most amazing person I ever knew and was my everything for as long as I knew him. Tell him I wish he'd come back, even just to say to say hello, or goodbye, or that it was nice to know me too. Tell him I will remember him as a good thing, and he changed my life forever. Tell him it was not the worst thing that happened to me, and that he is not my mistake, as I am his. Tell him I loved him so much.

Tell him I still love him.

Tell him I love him.

Do you remember him, or is he someone who you never knew at all?

CHAPTER EIGHTEEN

THE ROAD I'M ON

I have noticed, today—and other days, but today enough to make me think about it more—that strangers are so often kinder than friends and those who we love. My new market trader friends have shown kindness in small but touching ways—a cup of coffee from Computer-fixing Man; thoughts of comforting angels from Cupboard-under-the-stairs Mystic-Meg Lady; infinite small purchases from my stall, and sympathy for my 'plight'. The sympathy is usually unnamed but seems to cover all bases, from the failed business interpretation or the interpretation that is closer to my heart but was an unintentional insight; the loss of my partner. Partners, even. I could still have lost two of them; even I don't know yet exactly how careless I have been of my marriage. I should be amused that they have no clue who I really am—how can they, when I have no clue myself who I really am? I could be anyone or no one. I could be whoever I wanted to be, if only I knew who that was, or if others would play their roles in that option. Yesterday evening, I felt like no one at all—small, lost, and insignificant in my ability to change anything, but significant in the destruction I bring to those around me.

The first incident of the day's random kindnesses from random strangers was brought about by none of my new market-trader friends, but by Lovely-lorry-driver. It was, for a pleasant change, a beautiful morning—no ice on the windscreen to send my organised and leaving-on-time morning into a chaos of defrosting, no fog, and, unbelievably, no rain either. Just a stunning sunrise and a haze of orange glow. Unfortunately, and ungrateful of me to say so, the sunrise was shining straight at me and zapping my concentration as I squinted against it. Luckily, I was not too squinty to notice the mad flashing of Lovely-lorry-driver's lights as I touched the speedometer up over eighty. Fortunately, I was not lacking concentration to the point of not interpreting Lovely-flashing-lorry-driver as a warning to slow down. Luckily, therefore, as the speed camera van appeared in my vision, I was maintaining a safe and steady fifty-five miles per hour. Orange; hazy; still a beautiful morning, and no speeding fine either.

It impresses me that not only would he be thoughtful enough to warn me, but that he could tell my excessive speed, despite my driving in the opposite direction and passing him in the flash of a heartbeat. Someone else, who, after impacting on my life in a good way, I may never see again.

Even if I do, I will not recognise him as the man I met the first time.

Although I am a grownup—nearly forty, feeling every second of those years and wishing I really did feel like a grownup—I am still scared of so many things. Being heartbroken forever is one of those things. Not knowing who I am is another. Yet another is thinking someone was someone, then realising they are not. But yesterday, the thing that scared me most was being a passenger in a friend's car in Dublin.

"Come to Dublin for the day," Liz had urged. "It'll do you good."

I won't exaggerate, but I genuinely thought it was more likely to kill me. The idea of a day out was welcome relief; we could go Christmas shopping, get lunch, have some fun. James was home and could pick up the children; I could buy him something special to remind us both that I do still love him. Liz knew how much I needed a day away, but she couldn't know how much I hate her driving. I have driven in London and Manchester and around the big, scary edges of Birmingham, and on many motorways in England, and, way back when, I even *lived* in a city. But now . . . now I am scared of driving on any road busier than the one that leads from my house to the nearest town. I don't like driving in the town when I do get there, and the nearest town would still only count as a large village in the world I used to live in, back in England when I was years younger, but more grown up.

To be fair to Liz, we had a lovely day. We arrived safely in Dublin and enjoyed the shops and the busyness and anonymity of being in the city. We spent several hours weaving around crowds of other shoppers, ducking in and out of shops, throwing spare change to buskers, and singing along to cheesy Christmas music. We stopped in Bewley's for hot chocolate, and I felt a small but definite flutter of excitement about Christmas. We flirted with market traders, bought loads of Christmas presents, and stumbled, laden with shopping bags, into a pub in Temple Bar for lunch. I didn't think of Charles so much, but I did buy James a shirt I knew he'd love, and some of his favourite sweets. I bought some computer games for our son, and some pretty things I knew would make our daughter smile.

And then Liz drove us home. There are streets in Dublin where the road markings seem to have been painted by the traffic line painter's daughter, who is clearly only three and a half. And will need glasses before she is four. Some lines wriggle and swerve, some begin but end before they get anywhere they meant to go, and other lines steer you onto the wrong side of traffic islands and bollards so suddenly that you know you must be on the wrong side of the road, except you actually are not. Then, there are the lines and the lanes clearly based on my current life: these lanes disappear as soon as I get into them.

Every lane we are in, we are directed to move out of, just seconds after we were sign-posted to get into it. Every arrow on the road surface is curved towards any other lane but the one we are in, and when we get into the lane the curvy arrow told us to, the next arrow curves us straight back again. It must be an oxymoron that the curve sends us straight back, but this road is made up entirely of oxymorons. I can't help Liz by navigating, as I neither know Dublin, nor know how to interpret these road signs that don't help us drive the route we think we are on. I do know, as we battle through it, cutting corners, cutting up other drivers, dodging in front, leaping across lanes, and trying to avoid every other rush hour driver who is fighting the same fight, that this is an exact roadmap of my whole life. I was on a path, and now the signs are all mixed up. Nothing makes any sense, and I cannot tell where I came from, or where I am going. On this Dublin road, at a crazy time of night, I cannot find my way back to where we came from, and I cannot find a way forward. It is simply getting darker and more confusing. I don't say it aloud, but I am scared.

The drive home overshadows the excitement I'd felt earlier in the day—the fun of the shopping and the new-found anticipation of the approaching festive season. Although the day out with Liz had offered some respite from my constant state of confusion, that respite evaporates as soon as I sit in her passenger seat in the chaos of Dublin's rush hour.

We do find our way through eventually, and I do survive, but, as I was only ever the passenger, the decisions about how we got out of that place were never my own decisions.

CHAPTER NINETEEN

SOUNDTRACK

$\mathcal{T}$oday, I have moved on from chicklit or Victoriana and am running my life to an eighties' soundtrack. I don't mind this so much; as James tells people often, I'm an eighties' girl. He means that, in his opinion, I have no musical taste and know no music beyond 1987. To me, it simply reinforces exactly why I feel at home at the market. I am under the speaker and under the heater, and it feels like being on holiday. I could almost work on my tan, to the soundtrack of my life, which is mostly '80's songs that I know all the words to, and every lyric is talking either to me or about me. Tracks from the '60s or '70s pepper the '80's music every now and again and lull me to a childhood of nothing to worry about but the anticipation of what life will bring. Today, the melancholy hits me round about "Lean on Me," when there is a let-up in shoppers, and I can stop to catch my thoughts. It has been a long day of telling many people who I sort of know that, no, my other business is no longer running, and no, although Christmas is coming, Santa won't be coming to our Santa events this year, as there will be no Santa events at the cabins in the woods this year.

I tell the adults one story, and the children another. If I know the adults well, they get a slightly different version to those I know less. Some, who live close enough, and know us all, jump to the 'recession is so tough' conclusion, and I let them have that belief. Others get the 'my business partner is an ass' story. A select few get the raw heartache of my pain because they know me well enough to know it's there. One or two even may get the nearly true version, where Isobel has decided she "doesn't want me around anymore," but I give no one the whole truth, complete and unabridged. I wonder how many know it or guess it anyway. One woman, to whom I have already told, "He pulled out abruptly, suddenly, and horribly, and my heart is broken over it," returns later with her children, so I give them the "We just weren't making enough money and Charles needed to do some other work," version instead. The mother catches my eye and transmits such sympathy that I nearly cry all over again, for she clearly sees inside me that this is not easy for me at all.

I hate this transition from running a business that had massive success selling childhood dreams to adults and children alike, to having to explain to the same children that we can no longer afford childhood. We had created Christmas movie-worthy events filled with happy children, fortuitously well-timed real snowfalls, and Christmas cheer for the past two Christmases, and it was the single most successful thing we had done in terms of media response, follow-up, and paid articles. That first Christmas guaranteed our regular section in the weekend magazine of one of Ireland's 'better' newspapers, and it was easily my favourite event to run and document. And now I stand here in the market, trying to hold back my own tears while I make small children cry as I tell them our Christmas at the farm is cancelled.

The stress of being lost in Dublin yesterday brought me

home exhausted and tearful and unreasonably bad-tempered, and my own children already know that, for the time being, childhood is on hold while I fret about how to compensate for my lost income. My children, like James, are blaming Charles. I know I have let them do this by telling them that my business is gone because he pulled out—which is, at least, true—but is it fair to paint him as the only bad guy here? I can't care too much about that right now, as he has given me little other option. The truth is banned and the lies don't ring true, so this half-truth is all I have to offer to my children, and whilst they may not completely buy into it, they rarely question me for a more believable answer. My daughter often bursts out with, "Why did Charles do that?" but my son— almost an adult, infinitely wiser than his sister, and more scared of the truth than she is old enough to be—asks nothing at all.

Another friend visits my stall, and also asks nothing, for which I am grateful. Her standards of morality are clearly higher than mine, and if she were to ask out loud the questions to which she already knows the answer, and I were to answer her with the truth, then she, too, would feel it necessary to 'unfriend' me, and I would have lost yet another friend to the battlefield I have created. I feel friendless enough, with the loss of Charles and Isobel, so I truly appreciate that I mean enough to this friend for her not to ask, in order to remain my friend. In response, and in acknowledgement of how much I need her friendship, I do not tell her. Instead, we discuss dogs and weather and children and aging parents, but never the end of my business or the mutual friend we once had in Isobel. Some signs are still clear enough to understand, even if they are not written out.

Which reminds me again how he once looked at me as if

he loved me, and that it was clear enough to believe it without being spoken aloud or written down.

So here I am, under the speaker in the market, listening to Bill Withers with tears falling down my cheeks. His lyrics resonate through my very soul, and I remember how many times, so many times, we leant on each other. I so much want to remind Charles that I am his friend—I want him to lean on me; I want to help him carry on—yet he is the one who doesn't want to listen. And James—James who so desperately needs to hear it from me—is not the one I will say it to. And, as I stand in the market, wiping tears from my face and pretending to my customers that I am not crying, I am wondering how it has come to be that the only person I want to lean on is the one who is no longer available to me, but who it felt so very right to lean into and against and on, and whose arms I felt at home in.

CHAPTER TWENTY

DAYS LIKE THESE

I watch as the little yellow car in front of me ignores the red traffic light at the roadworks and drives on through. The digger swings, but misses it. I do that thing where I tell the driver what I think of him. (Or her? Surely not.) I have a little rant to myself, because I am the only one who listens to me anyway, and I wonder out loud how people can be so stupid. The light goes green, so I follow the yellow car through. Just at the end of the roadworks, a digger is neatly parked all the way across the entrance to the garage. My petrol light insists I need to turn in anyway, so I enter through the exit instead. I swing around to the only possible pump I will be able to manoeuvre back out of, given the position of the digger, and curse at the switched-off pump.

It turns out to be a good thing that the pump is off, as I then notice it is kerosene anyway. I guess that's why it isn't left turned on—to avoid dozy drivers like me from filling diesel engines with kerosene. The pump next to it says DIESEL, in clear, big letters. So, there I am, nozzle in hand, nozzle in diesel tank, watching the gauge tick round and chatting to the elderly assistant as he leans on a broom to take time to catch his breath. Kindness of strangers clearly spills into this village I am passing through, for every time I am here, people are chatty and friendly and pass the time of day. Nonetheless, they do not help me with my directions. I am lost—although I know exactly where I am, I do not know where I am going—and the friendly man cannot give me the directions I need to stop me from driving in circles. His random friendliness quickly turns into dire warning as he points out that I am happily pumping green diesel. Green diesel, he reminds me, is for farm traffic and is illegal to use on the road in domestic vehicles. I have just become a criminal.

"Might as well carry on, now you've started," the old man acknowledges.

We laugh about the potential fine, a penalty for a genuine mistake I feel guilty for. As I attempt to pick my way blindly past the digger, complete with my illegal tank of green stuff, I wonder if it is really green and if I will puff a trail of green smoke from my exhaust to tell the world (and the police) that I am a cheat, a thief, and a chancer. The digger driver backs up, lifts his shovel, and waves me out, and I drive all the way to where I should be going without being apprehended by anyone who gets suspicious about my hypothetical puffs of green smoke.

A very suspicious noise, however, comes from the engine, or some other generic part of the car. My usual way of dealing with this kind of strange noise is to turn up the radio. The farther I drive, the louder I turn the radio, and the noise is particularly bad when I brake or turn left.

I realise that, in some areas, I am remarkably able to bury my head firmly in the sand, and that is just one of a trillion indications that Charles are I are a perfect match. He is the king of head-buriers, and I am sure he still has his head firmly in very deep, very sticky sand, where I assume it will remain until Isobel gives him permission to remove it. Maybe I should help her to hold it down instead. I need to start to hate him for his part in this mess; to make him take some share of the blame and the pain. Maybe I don't need to; without the ability to act of his own free-will, consequently, I suppose, his head will remain in sand until he suffocates without help from either me or Isobel. I think I may have passed him, driving his mother's car, as he and his brother often do. I can't be sure if it was him, as thoughts of yellow cars, diggers, and illegal fuel are distracting me. Many similar cars are on the roads, and many members of his family drive that car, if it even is the right car. If it is him, he doesn't wave. In fairness, if it isn't him, then the driver who isn't him also doesn't wave.

I don't understand how he doesn't wave anymore when he passes me on the road. Perhaps it is my bad eyesight that means I always wave first before checking it is someone I actually know. But, aside from that, if you have automatically waved at someone's car for four years, it must be a conscious decision to force yourself to not wave—and a quick-thinking decision at that, I wonder if he starts to wave, but catches himself in time. Perhaps I am so well blanked from his memory that he truly does not recognise me, even though I drive an eye-dazzlingly garish car that has my name written on it, for business reasons. I suppose I must consider changing it, now that my business is no longer what it used to be. Charles has driven this car so often himself that he would never not recognise it. On this day, I will give benefit of doubt, and believe it was not him who did not wave or pass me on the road.

The rust and the rattle and the diesel and changing the decals are problems I cannot afford to deal with today, for I still have no job, no income of my own to contribute to our household expenses, and my new life as a market trader has limited days, as business has become slow, and the traders are worried.

I have the germ of an idea shaping slowly through the fog in my head, and maybe it will become a future, or maybe I am too scared and too burnt and too tired to dream anymore. I know I have limited resources, and dreams are now beyond realistic hope when they are business dreams that require funding, backing, business plans, and trust. Definitely beyond hope if they need trust. I like the market, and I like the idea of learning to be a shop-girl, but I cannot afford shop fittings, and I cannot afford trust. I can't really afford dreams, but sometimes they come anyway, even if I don't invite them.

As far as I know, there is a French lesson for my daughter and Charles's tonight. It has been two weeks since his eldest daughter called me to say the lesson was cancelled, but I've heard nothing to suggest we shouldn't go tonight. I assume that when I arrive, he will have the curtains shut and the television turned up loud, to drown out the rattle of my failing brakes and the rattle of emptiness in his kitchen while I sit in my car outside in the cold and the dark. I still long to sit inside with my friend and share tea and stories and hopes and dreams, while we allow our children these lessons of normality, because it is easier to continue them than to tell our children who we really are. However, he will pretend I am not there, and I will pretend not to dream or remember or hope or wonder.

Undeniably, we will both know I am there, and that he is there, and that both our 'theres' are separated only by my car window and his house window—and the very thick, very dark, very heavy curtain he has drawn between us.

I am not so un-generous that I cannot allow that maybe the driver of the red-light-jumping yellow car of this morning has other things on their mind too. Perhaps their car has a worrying rattle on braking or turning left. Perhaps they are sick, or tired, or someone they know has died. Perhaps they, too, have a broken heart to distract them at every moment of every day, and every action makes them remember things someone else wants to forget. The yellow car driver is maybe not stupid, or a cheat or a chancer; she probably just has a mind that takes her to a million other places she would rather be, or once was able to go.

(He? Surely not.)

When spring comes around again, he won't have an excuse to draw the curtains anymore, and maybe my days will be brighter.

CHAPTER TWENTY-ONE

GRIEF AND LOSS

mutual friend has died. He was a close friend of Charles and Isobel. To me, he was someone I knew through them, whose wife had become a friend and sometimes-colleague. I haven't heard from her in the aftermath of Isobel discovering I wanted to break her marriage and take her husband away, and I know she is the one person who Isobel turned to. I know she will be distraught and grief-stricken at this sudden death of her husband, but undoubtedly strong and dignified too. They seemed to be the ultimate picture of a couple growing old together, projecting an image—outwardly, at least—of peace, calm, and wisdom. Now, for her, she must endure the infinite sadness of having to carry on without her partner. James used to have an album with the title, *Melancholy and the Infinite Sadnesss,* and I never really understood what that meant until now. That, at least, is something I have learned in the past few months, because we—James and I—live under a cloud of infinite sadness now.

The days have been so dark this week—barely scraping daylight, and a constant need for headlights and torches and coats. I am having a much-needed catchup day. The kiln is firing, and I can only wait for it. The house is screaming for attention; the washing is piled in confused tangles of dry, nearly dry, and still so damp it will soon need washing again. I had planned to take Jess on a long and purposeful walk. I thought of walking farther into the village (and nearer to Charles), but now it is raining, which won't stop me, but I have an at-home child. She is not sick, but exhausted by school and dullness and times tables. Her definition of a good or a bad day has become the same as mine: whether she cried or not. She is too young to be dragged down by this life, and I worry about her. I must drag myself out of this sadness and start being her mother again. I must. She is having a do-whatever-she-likes day, but I know, at some stage, it will become dictated by me, be it a demand for shared dog-walking, or a need to escape the house, or a request for help with something. For now, I will try to leave her until I can make time for fun.

The new idea is still gnawing at the corners of my mind, but I am scared to think it through. No, I am not scared to think it through, rather, I am excited to *think* it through. It is following it through, acting upon it, taking it further, that scares me, for it will involve trust, commitment, confidence, self-belief, and, of course, finance—of which I also have none, even if the other things on the list were spilling from me in abundance. There is an empty shop unit not far away, that I pass often, which triggers absent-minded thoughts. I could do so much with it. It is a perfect space (probably not a perfect location, but a good enough one). I could put in a small coffee-shop, an art workshop space, a gallery or studio, or both—a small gift area, and art and craft supplies. I could add sofas and make a safe space. People could call in to knit, to chat, to buy, to drink coffee, to try a new activity, to make something, to create, to explore, to try. To do *something*. My phoenix will grace the signage in full glory, and I will rise from the darkness and be somebody who does something. It will be slow—I am, at least, realistic—but it will work, and people will like it and come for friendship as well. I will show the world that the recession will bring out the good in people, and we will learn to do new things, or relearn how to do the old things, and we will not be beaten by the recession. There is enough else trying to beat us without the recession needing to win.

James could help me. We could do it together.

I even took down the phone number, from where it hung, beckoning, on the doorway of the empty shop, stuck by peeling Sellotape and hope. But I am afraid to call it, for then it becomes something more real than just a dream. I am too tired to try to make my dreams real again. I did that before. I am too scared to be in business with anyone else. I did that before too. I am stuck in 'once bitten, what the hell now?' and too frightened to love and lose, too scared to believe in a dream or in myself. I am too scared to start something new and move away from the therapy I find in making things from thumping clay.

Actually, I am learning to be gentler with the clay. Too many pieces have warped this time and have been smashed into crumbs to recycle later when I have the energy or the anger to thump really, really hard and reform those broken pieces into workable clay. I am learning that some things cannot be moved or disturbed, but must be left patiently, watched carefully, so they are only lifted before they are too dry but not when they are so wet that they will twist. I must leave my clay pieces to dry in a cooler place than the kitchen table, and I must become more patient. I need to pay more attention to timing and stages and processes, then my pieces will not frustrate me as they twist and bend.

I must be gentle and not rough or bad-tempered.

I talked to Charles the other day. This is how I know the friend has died. I lied to James again and let him think Charles had called me with the news. I phoned Charles. Just about the French lessons, nothing else. Not to hear his voice or talk to him or check if he has blocked me on his phone, as well as on Facebook. Not for any of those reasons. We were civil, and pleasant. For a moment. He told me that since we were talking on the phone, he "might as well tell me" that his friend is dead, as if even to share news of a death of a friend is taboo and dis-allowed. "Might as well tell me." I conclude from that statement that Charles would not, as James thinks, have been "good to tell me," had I not called him first.

Charles also told me that he thinks the children's French lessons must end soon, in the office space at the farm, at least. I can, of course, have the university student come to my own house to teach my own children, as I want. He gives me permission for that as if he has that level of control over us all. He does not want our children sharing even a French lesson, but he especially does not want them to share our old office space, where the lessons take place. He wants to put order back into his life. He wants to use the space for something else. He wants to move on. I am between amused and angered that the lessons between our children, which they need and enjoy, which remind them of the time they were like siblings, must end so he can have order in his life. I try to contain my anger, so the conversation can continue. I need to hear his voice.

I ask him instead how he is. He says he is fine.

The conversation spirals downwards when I revisit discontinuing the French lessons, and we end on a low note. I am no longer even partially amused, and the glimpse of good humour has left my day.

Later, much later, I realise he cannot be fine. I discover through mutual friends that Isobel is away, in another country, on her own, while their friend is dead. Charles cannot be fine. I want to offer support in the absence of Isobel. Because, for four years, I could support and comfort and listen and talk and offer friendship when his wife could not; and now, perhaps at the exact moment he needs it most, I am not able to. I store the knowledge that she has gone away, for I am not sure what it means. To me, it will probably mean nothing, and if she leaves for good, it will cause him to blame me and hate me for all the things he already blames and hates me for. He has forgotten, I think, that the blame is shared. I know he needs a friend, and I know it cannot be me. Another germ of an idea crawls uninvited into the area of my mind where the ridiculous and the sublime ideas live: Dial-a-friend—a bit like the Samaritans, but you send out a friend to chat to, drink tea with, talk about everything and nothing; it's like a pizza delivery, except it talks to you.

I wonder who he makes tea for now in the way he made it for me. I like to think he uses a spoon for the tea bag with anyone else. For me, he would use his fingers, which I came to see as intimate rather than lazy or unhygienic or just plain wrong. I loved the intimacy of that, and I never saw him do it with anyone else's tea. If I was allowed to go in for tea now, I wonder if he would use a spoon. I miss taking his own cup from his hand and drinking from it. Sometimes I would arrive in the mornings, and he would already have a cup of tea that he was drinking, and I would reach for the cup and share it, as if it were my own.

The funeral of the friend will take place in his homeland, abroad, and far away. I had a flash of a vision that if it were here, Isobel would stand beside her friend in the absence of family who are all abroad, and when condolences were offered, I would hug the widow with all my heart and soul, then I would look Isobel in the eyes and say how very, very sorry I am for her loss too, for I know exactly how it feels to lose a friend.

I realise that whenever we talk on the phone, it doesn't go well, and I cannot control my emotion, so I write him a letter instead.

Dear Charles,

I am bewildered by the fact that every time we talk, my emotions overrule, and the conversation turns to tears and anger and being upset. So, I will not speak. I understand you cannot talk to someone who cries every time a conversation starts. What I should have said on Monday was how sorry I am for your loss, for I know how hard it is to lose a friend, and I realise now your wife is away, and you may have no one to offer you comfort. I know you told me that you are fine, and you want me to believe that, but to lose a close friend and to be alone to deal with it is not easy, even if you didn't have a thousand other emotions to deal with right now. You will not allow it, but I would make tea and offer friendship if you would let me. I can be your friend without it being about love or sex or betrayal or pain. I can be your friend, because someone has died, and it is okay to be sad, but it's hard to be sad alone.

CHAPTER TWENTY-TWO

AWAY

*E*verybody has those days that begin with the realisation that the dishwasher didn't wash properly. Everybody must have days that begin with the necessity of washing by hand last night's baked-on dinner that has successfully managed the drying cycle but is not clean. This is the stage set for this whole new day—chasing my tail and completing jobs I had expected to be done already. I wonder though, does this really happen to us all, or is that like saying everybody will wake up one morning, and it will be the day when they fall in love with their friend, who is married to their other friend, and who is clearly not their own husband, as he is safely at home, getting on with loving her and living his marriage, just as he always has, with no thought of anyone else being a part of it?

Isobel has fled across the sea to her homeland. My overactive mind tells me she is running, hiding, assessing, and, probably by this time, seeking solace and comfort by spilling her story to old friends and closest family. I cannot believe it is coincidence that she is gone at this time, and my

racing brain can imagine the whole new life she has mapped
out for herself. Even now, she is probably meeting with the
people from real estate, window shopping for the setting for
her own next chapter. She will look at townhouses, in
suburban lanes, or city streets, surrounded by buzz and life
and noise. This will distract her better than calm country and
fields, as country life would remind her of what she used to
have here before I destroyed it for her.

She will have a neat and tidy house, and things and
furnishings will match and be stored in exactly their right
places. There will never be dust. I know her energy and focus
will be in putting order into her new home, in a desperate
attempt to put order into her life. It will be a far cry from the
disordered home she lives in now, which is untidy but feels
like home. She will live the American dream. My imagination
stalls as I can't imagine who will go with her to this new life
across the ocean, far from friends, family, and farm life. The
oldest girl will refuse to go. She is nearly grown and is
comfortable in her world, so, she will hate me for forcing the
choice between her parents and her countries and her siblings.
The middle child will be torn beyond even that. She has a
thousand friends here and is popular and loved, but is secretly
insecure and will not want to start over in a country where her
peers will be a million times more sophisticated than her. But
she will not want to be without her mother, and she will hate
me for forcing a choice on her she cannot make. As for the
youngest, I cannot decide in any fantasy mapping of anyone's
future life whether she would go or stay. I think Isobel would
take her with her. Surely, she would not leave her. So ... so,
then she has lost the father who adores her and whom she
adores, and who has given her so much and who has made
her who she is. She will not hate me, because she will

remember she loved me, but I will hate myself for tearing apart her family and ripping her away from her sisters and her father.

Or maybe ... maybe the unthinkable will come to pass. He will go with them all, and they will start again as a unit, building a new life in a new country where everything is fine. The stick-on smiles of photographs will become the expressions they wear every day. In their new American life, they will convince themselves everything is just fine and nothing bad ever happened to any of them.

I think I still know him well enough to see it could never last. He would miss his own family in Ireland, and his land and the outdoors. The city would stifle him, and the cracks would turn into canyons the size of the one that destroyed our own relationship. Then I remember I do not know him at all anymore, and he is no longer the person I thought I knew. He has become a stranger, and only when I look into his eyes, or hear a fleeting moment of something that used to be there in his voice, do I still believe I know him so well.

I wonder how many houses she has looked at, and how soon she can begin her new American life. How fast can she uproot her children, whether by taking them or by leaving them? Although my heart aches for her and the decisions she will make, I know that really my heart only aches for me. By the time his family is ripped asunder, he will hate me too. He has, by now, forgotten the part he had to play in getting us all to this point. How will he ever remember he loved me if all he can do is hate me and blame me for everything that has changed for him? I want to put my arms around him and tell him everything will be fine, but as long as I feel the need to put my arms around him, nothing will be fine for any of us.

I wonder if her children know she is planning her escape

and theirs. Do they know she is away, planning how to rebuild a new life from the remnants of her old one I have left her with? Do they think she is simply visiting friends and family and elderly parents? It is not beyond possibility that she is *actually* visiting friends and family and elderly parents. Maybe there is a wedding or a funeral or a new baby or a sick aunt or something important that had to be done and she is not planning an escape at all. I, of course, prefer to imagine that her marriage is falling apart, for that gives me hope of seeing him again, in time. I know when he has remembered we were closer to each other than anyone else ever was— when he has forgotten he hates me and blames me and that we destroyed our worlds—then he will call me back to him.

Although I loved him too much to stop it, it bothered me immensely that he was married to my friend. He told me once, when I voiced this, that he suspects it is "quite common." He is probably right, given that our friends are the people we like the most. It follows that now and again, perhaps we fall in love with them too. And except for the whole falling in love with her husband thing, I was a good friend to her, and I was kind, and I was respectful of the difficulty of running my business from her home. I tried so hard to consult her on anything and everything that would impact on her life.

Except for the one big thing that would impact her life to such an extent it would damage it forever.

Except for that, I was her friend.

For James and Charles, too, there was, whilst not exactly friendship, a male bonding of shared power tools and help with lifting things or fixing things. A certain level of trust existed, although Isobel questioned this more often than James, and, over time, became increasingly resentful of the excess of time I spent with her husband. But even now, as her friend, I want to say to her that Charles was right; it happens to lots of people, and it has happened to us. I want to say to her that running away to a new life won't change it. I try not to allow jealous thoughts to creep in—*at least she has the money to run away across the sea*—and I try not to wish too hard that I, too, could run away across the sea, if only I had a job to pay for it.

In the time since more people have become aware of what I have done, I have heard that many of them have done it too. I have friends or family in every corner of the world who have had some experience of a similar heart-breaking, family-destroying, life-changing story disguised as love but ending as hate and betrayal. Across the same sea, also in the States, my cousin's marriage is falling apart. We are the same age, Alice and I, and despite the distance of miles between us, we have been close throughout our lives. Recently, our childhood habit of letter writing has given way to adult Facebook chat. I am stunned to hear that in her far-away life, she has become Isobel. Her long-time husband has "taken up" with her oldest childhood friend. She is bewildered and distraught. She does not know what to do with this betrayal, and she cannot yet believe it.

I can only say, "I believe it." I believe it, for I am that friend, who has done the same thing, to Isobel, and with Charles. Alice knows this. I have written to her many times over the past year or so. She knows what I have done, and she knows Isobel was my friend. All I can say is, "It happens." She is beginning to believe it because I am the proof. Despite having no sympathy for her own friend or her husband, she is spilling over with sympathy for me.

I wonder whether Isobel would be sympathetic to me if it were anyone else I had fallen in love with. Either way, I feel a need to say to her, however far she runs or wherever she runs to, it will always be the same. Even across the sea, even in her own safe homeland, someone somewhere is sleeping with their friend's husband, or their wife's friend. She can't hide from this. It is strange how I am still so shocked to hear of every other story.

As the friend I used to be to her, before I wanted to take her husband for my own, I want to warn her:

Dear Isobel,

Even over there in your homeland, in America, Land of the Free, you are not safe from cheats and liars. They are in every corner of the world. Even there, even where you feel safe on your home ground, there will be men who 'take up' with their wife's friend, and break hearts, and make promises and break them as quickly. For when one promise is kept, another is broken.

I want to warn her also that, if, as she seems to want to hear and Charles seems to want to say, it all meant nothing to him at all, then,

Dear Isobel, dear, dear Isobel, **surely, if it meant nothing, he will do it again.**

I believe it is better to risk everything for someone who means everything than to risk everything for nothing—for a mistake. I became my best friend's biggest mistake, for which he has said he is sorry, but sorry, by that point, is just another empty promise.

Dear Isobel,

If he could hold me in his arms and tell me how much he loved you; if he could kiss me; and tell me how much he

loved you; if he could take me in his arms after a weekend
away with you, kiss me, hold me, touch me, and tell me his
weekend with you has shown him how much he still loved
you, then why, oh why was he holding me in his arms?

It is not impossible to want it all.

CHAPTER TWENTY-THREE

MISSING ANGELS

*T*he angels in my marketplace are gone today. The cupboard-under-the-stairs Mystic-Meg angel has given up and moved out. I wonder if she saw that coming when, last week, she seemed so sure she would stay? She was encouraging and friendly and impressed by my making of angels in the face of adversity, and she believed instantly in my strength and determination and the ability to go on. I was tempted to sit in her cupboard and hear her take on the tarot of my life. In my mind, her fortune-telling skills predicted a happy ending and a love story, but then the devil on my shoulder reminded me that my cards may show nothing but darkness and loss. And that is not what I want to know.

My daughter was also tempted by a happy ending scenario, where she is predicted to be living with wolves in a feral wolf-child story. But, like me, she was too scared to hear reality, where her life is not the storybook she wants but the one in which the wolves are hungry and eat the innocent at every opportunity. Her fascination with wolves is incomprehensible, even to my twisted imagination. In my story, they prey on girls in forests and lure them into clearings, hollows, grassy banks, and against trees on tangled paths. In my story, they are temptation with irresistible lures. They are baited with looks of love that are only a disguise for feral instinct and basic lust. In her child's mind, a wolf is friendly, grey, loyal, soft, and strong. In my nearly forty-year-old head, he used to be all that, but it was only a disguise for the animal underneath that ate me alive and spat out my soul.

The other angel missing from the market today is one from the other end of the room. She massaged my shoulders and my back, and my head and my arms. I went to her for a hope of relief from an old injury, and she found emotional stress weighing more heavily on my shoulders than any real injury was causing. She remembered after starting my shoulder massage that I had told my story of a failed partnership, and she was one of the traders who I had thought had got the story wrong. The weight of the world on my shoulders burnt a shadow her hands could feel, and she tried to drain it through my arms towards the floor. The sceptic in me gave way to the dark swirls of red and black my mind conjured, interspersed with the babble of the marketplace outside the flimsy curtain. The sceptic in me popped its head back up to assume the darkness swirling into brighter blues and calmer colours in my mind was my imagination trying desperately to clear my mind. I wondered—even as I was being told to relax; pummelled into relaxing; stroked into relaxing; therapy-ed into relaxing—whether I am the only person who works so hard at trying to relax that I cannot relax in case I forget I am trying to. Either way, this masseuse angel felt my pain and told me to lose it.

Necessary by now to admit it is not my husband who has left me floundering, but a failed business and lost friendship, she again wrong-footed me by saying she heard it right the first time. Then she assured me that I am better alone. Now I cannot tell whether she means alone in business, work, future career, and money-making plans, or alone in my marital bed. I cannot ask, for I am afraid of the answer.

⁓

Dear Isobel,

I wonder if we are thinking similar thoughts right now. We must both resent each other. We are both unsure of whether we want to be alone or with our own husbands. We both wonder if we want to be with your husband. We are uncertain of the future and wish each other would leave our lives to make room for the rest of our life to carry on. You want me out of your life, so you can have a fighting chance to rebuild it. With your husband. I want you out of mine to see if there is any hope that, without you, he would choose me. If it were not me who had done this to you and not you who has all that I want, we would talk to each other and cry together, and hope and dream . . .

⁓

Dear Isobel

I know you think I am a despicable person, but I didn't ever plan to hurt you. While my angels have gone missing this week, I hope yours are watching over you. But I still hope they tell you that you are better alone.

There are always so many words I do not send. I wonder, will she listen to the angels if they tell her she is better alone? I have no doubt that while she is away, she is looking for angels. I wonder though what it is she wants them to tell her. I have met some of her friends and family. Some will tell her to leave him; some will tell her to stay. Most of them will tell her I am the bad guy. I cannot guess whether any of them will remember that he is the bad guy too, and I suspect most of them will suggest she runs me down in the street. I am not sure anyone will tell her to run him down or out.

It has been a pleasant change to walk Jess without thinking she will drive by and run me down, but that relief is coupled with knowing that if I see her car this week, it will be him driving it, so now I look harder and walk for longer, just in case he passes by.

It is strange to have known so much about her for so long but to not know when she will be home; I wonder if Charles knows when she is coming home. I wonder if it is 'if' and not 'when'.

Not only were my angels missing, but the '80's soundtrack I had already got used to was gone this week too. That American influence is still trying its hardest to get under my skin to irritate and unnerve me. American radio throbs into the speaker above my market stall, pulsing with gangster rap and insults. It is wholly inappropriate for family shopping on a rainy November Saturday, but strangely calming to me; for once, not every lyric is directed straight to my heart. Today, this repetitive loop of abuse and put-your-hands-over-your-children's-ears lyrics is a refreshing escape from broken hearts, love, and loss. The lunchtime switch to Christmas songs is relaxing too, if a little early. I feel old in my admission that I would have been happier with Christmas carols than the tedious strains of *"Santa baby, coming down my chimney tonight."* Carols, at least, would have conjured childhood nostalgia of a time before heartbreak—a time when the hardest thing in life was sleepily going home from midnight mass, wondering whether Santa had made it down our own chimney yet. "Santa Baby" just reminds me that sleaze is everywhere, even, or especially, at Christmastime.

And instantly, all my thoughts return to Charles. There is a vivid flash of memory of our eyes burning into each other with a clichéd electricity I can't believe anyone in the same room could have missed on Christmas Eve two years ago when nothing had happened yet and everything was still going to.

How different Christmas will be now. Even last year, as we hugged, briefly alone, and intimate, I know he thought I was going to kiss him. I wonder over and over whether, on that occasion, he might have let me. I wonder too if he was disappointed I didn't even try. He carefully avoided me for the rest of the night while I talked in the kitchen with Isobel, pretending we were still as close as we used to be, before she became resentful of the time I spent with her husband and before I proved her right to resent me.

Nonetheless, I still want to believe in the fairy tale of love and happiness and dreams coming true. I will thump my clay into princes and princesses this week, at the request of a customer. I will add a frog at the prince's feet to remind the princess of the consequences of taking a chance. Some you win; some turn out to be nothing but pond slime.

CHAPTER TWENTY-FOUR

MID-LIFE

*S*tereotypically, when men have their little mid-life crisis thing, it is clichéd beyond belief. They pretend it is nothing, or was nothing, or certainly will be nothing if they bury their head far enough. For the women I know who have gone through this, I notice they prefer to scream and shout, and rage and cry. Then they want to run away. They do this internally or externally, in public or in private. In my mind, I have run so far that I am still running. In real life, I am too tired and too scared and too broken to run anywhere, but, more than that, my children need me still, and I don't have any spare money to go anywhere anyway. Even if I could afford to, I won't become the mother who ran away. Whilst Isobel is running to her homeland and to time to think, Alice—my cousin whose husband has done to her what I have done to mine—is running this way. She is coming to seek solace and comfort, and to comfort and bring solace to me. I am not sure we will be good for each other.

We may not even know each other, Alice and I, for it has been half a lifetime since we last saw each other. We are rushing headlong towards forty, jaded and beaten, with our hearts in shreds. The last time we met, we had it all to look forward to. We were young, in love with our own husbands, and they with us. Our children were babies, or toddlers, or some of them not yet even born. We had hopes and dreams. We still had the future. We had a young, naïve confidence that the world was ours to do with as we pleased.

Now, more than fifteen years since we saw each other last, mostly I think we will cry, and although we will cry at the happiness of meeting again, we will cry more for why she is coming here. She will wish me to make it work with James, and, in return, I will tell her how despicable it is what her husband has done to her. The ridiculousness of us advising our own opposites will not be missed. This, of course, is assuming we recognise each other at the airport.

Dublin airport is small, and I think we will know each other by the lostness of ourselves mirrored in each other. The airport will be buzzing with people with tans from winter sun; sporty types laden with skis and snowboards, or families towing tired children, high on expensive airport food. There will be people with small briefcases and big suitcases, and people wearing impossibly high stiletto heels. If I were to try to be the kind of glamorous and worldly woman who could walk through airports in six-inch heels, I would only become the woman who got her shoe stuck in the escalator and had to go embarrassingly shoeless for the rest of her journey. Whoever I reinvent myself as now, it will not be that kind of woman.

Alice will arrive harassed and tired. I will be rushing to meet her, late and hassled by parking and buying strong coffee to keep myself awake long enough to tell her she must be tired. We will stand out in the crowd—to each other, at least. We will recognise each other from the hearts we wear on our sleeves and the souls that are broken in our eyes. We will politely exclaim, "You haven't changed at all!" while each thinking how old and tired we have become, and we will fall into each other's arms and hold on to each other as if we are drowning. We will have so much to talk about that we may not talk at all, and the balance of my children's Christmas holiday will be changed by the stranger in our midst.

I wonder if she is coming primarily to save me, to save herself, or to simply hide from the choices she needs to make. I wonder if making her choices will help me make mine or if my indecision and stuttering through my days will turn her further inside her own turmoil. How far our lives have come in all the years that have passed us by.

I hope she will offer some comfort to James whilst she is with us. They, at least, are in the same boat. Perhaps they will bond over this, fall in love. Perhaps she will bring him the gift of a second chance at life, and I will wish them well, hope they make it, and be grateful for the lifeline thrown so I can bail out. With this thought, I know my overactive imagination is getting carried away. A wing and a prayer are what I am wishing for, but I do not know where either one would need to take me for me to be happy.

Many thousands of hours ago, way back when my whole 'Spring of Hope' thing was going on with Charles, he referred to the fun we had whilst still testing the water of each other's reactions to our increasingly obvious feelings for each other. We spent such a long time testing the water. For a thousand years, I did not look up when we hugged. Although there had been moments of the warm, solid feel of his hands on my back, skin on skin, and hugs—so many hugs by then—we refused to acknowledge we would take it further, and I would not, could not, look up. I knew already that looking up at him would lead to that non-retractable, inevitable kiss. For months, I did not look up, and we held each other increasingly often, for many reasons and for no reasons. We hugged each other for reassurance after a difficult day, or for apology after a disagreement. We hugged for warmth after a day spent building fences in a snowstorm, or for a job done well or an exceptionally good photograph, or for security in doubt. We hugged because we could and because we wanted to.

It was the day of the snowstorm when the next line was crossed. The boundary we had set when we saw the way this was shaping up was that we would not kiss: no kissing, no sex. Those were the rules we set when it was first said aloud that we had this mutual attraction clearly and rapidly attacking our defences. No kissing. No sex. And for two months, we managed to keep the rules. Once the first rule was broken, the second was said louder, and again, and with genuine intent. It only lasted a matter of weeks, possibly only days, before that rule too, overtook us and our hands were in each other's clothes and ripping at each other's underwear and he was touching me where no one but James had touched me in years. That "no sex" rule crumbled into the dust at our feet and laughed at our naivety in thinking we could ever control the uncontrollable.

He was right; it was fun testing the water. The build up to even that first kiss was exciting. It was so very exciting. It was every inch of every nerve on tingling standby, tantalizing and expectant. The next three months did nothing to control that tingling anticipation. So why, then, after three months of the best time I ever had, did he suddenly realise the water was too damn hot? Surely testing it should've told him that. I thought he, too, had realised it felt exactly right and like a bath you could lie in forever, while you became wrinkled and relaxed and comfortable. If I have never felt so comfortable with anyone else, then how, please somebody tell me how, he suddenly found it too hot? Even if I understand him jumping out of the water so quickly once it started to burn him, I cannot understand how he left me in to drown.

I cannot understand how he could leave me to drown.

And I cannot understand why James still wants to be my lifeboat.

And I cannot understand how Alice thinks I can be hers.

I still cannot understand so much, and I cannot understand why he would not even say goodbye in the end. I am reminded again of the confusion of the road markings in Dublin. It made no difference which road we followed, for we were always in the wrong lane. And we would either get there, or we would end up somewhere else.

There are only two choices from here, and one is up, and one is down, and I want to go up—really, I do—but it is so much harder than going down.

CHAPTER TWENTY-FIVE

APRIL SHOWERS

I lose myself in the bathroom.

James often complains that I have the water far too hot. I may come out red and burned, but I like it hot. I like it hot, bubbly, and the door locked. I like it with a cup of tea, or, increasingly these days, a glass of red—a whole damn bottle of red, some days. I try to read, but, mostly, I drift. Tonight, as the bathwater steams around me, I lie dreaming of another bath time, way back when all the water was still inviting and before Charles realised he found it unbearably hot.

We were by the stream one day during that magical springtime, late into April, and it was so hot. I was lying on the grass on my tummy, watching the fish—sticklebacks, we called them as children—and wondered if these were the same kind. Charles muttered some 'proper' name for them—I've forgotten it now—and splashed water at my face. We giggled like children, and I commented that I could lie here in the sun, by the stream, for the rest of my life, and be quite content. We spent so much time by the stream. We would dress it up with 'work' that needed to be done—him fixing fences, clearing nettles, checking campfire sites; me following with the camera—but really, it was just the most peaceful place to be. It was acres from the house. It was out of view of the roads or neighbouring houses by several fields, and perfectly positioned on the edge of the wood to benefit from full sun all day long during that beautiful, sunny, spring. If no guests were occupying the cabins, it was entirely our own.

"What about Isobel?" I'd asked, early on, when we were nothing more than business partners on the brink of friendship. "Doesn't she ever come here?" All the years I spent working with Charles, I don't think I saw her here once. If she wanted to swim with the children, they preferred the deeper water of the woodland pool. It was both better for swimming, and nearer to the house. Isobel was too busy to spend her hours traversing endless fields for fun. I, however, ensured I was exactly busy enough to need to be in those same fields as often as possible.

"We should check the campfire pits daily in this heat," I said, embracing the excuse of the danger of hot embers spreading on the dry grass.

"We should clear out the spring. They'll be using it all the time in this weather," Charles might suggest other times.

"The nettles are beginning to get out of hand," I'd offer another day, and we'd strap the strimmers over our backs and set off across the farm. Using the strimmer made me feel like a Bond girl: all machinery and skimpy vest tops and well-fitting Levi's. I looked damn fine that spring, and I knew it. I had lost weight from the physical exertion of walking—running often—around the land, and from all the manual jobs Charles and I did daily. The sun had put a glow on my face and tanned my arms, and the glow from the sun covered the glow from being in love. I am fairly sure, even without sun, I would have glowed. I felt I looked awesome wielding the strimmer, an unusual confidence I had not experienced in as long as I could remember. I was encouraged in this vanity by the weight of Charles's gaze watching me if I walked ahead of him on the narrower pathways. I would stomp along the riverbank, swinging that strimmer from side to side, declaring war on nettles and unruly grasses, or sweep it in a wide arc reminiscent of a low-sweeping lightsaber attack as I cut a rough path across an open field. I liked it enough that I would often discard my camera, leave it far away and neglected in the office, even, in favour of the strimming work. Often, if Charles was busy elsewhere on the land, or inside the house with Isobel on a quiet Saturday, I would still pull on my walking boots, and set off, strimmer strapped across my body, hoping and hoping he would get away from whatever tedious thing was keeping him from me, and come and find me out on the land.

In the heat of that April, I would inevitably end up beside the stream, hot, sweaty, and covered in green stains and red scratches. It was far too hot to listen to James's advice to cover up when strimming—the jeans were already a compromise over cut-offs—and I wore the nettle debris and sharp remnants of severed stalks with the pride of a battle scar. *Look at me,* they said, *I am a capable, hard-working, power-tool wielding, Bond girl, and I can do anything. Anything.*

As the petrol ran low, I would inevitably turn towards the dip where the land met the water most easily, next to the freshwater spring, and collapse in an exhausted heap. I would pull off my top to shake out the grass, and splash water all over, to cool myself and to wash off the muck. Oftentimes, I would rinse my vest in the stream and lie back in the sun in my jeans and bra while my top lay steaming on the rocks beside me to dry. My tan did not stop at my shoulders that summer.

In the early part of April, I was careful to cover up if I heard Charles coming. Even in the days of our "kissing-but-no-further" rule, I was quick to pull on my top if he approached, but, by that particular day, as I lay on my tummy and tickled my hands through the stream and he threw water at me, it didn't seem to matter very much. The heat and the calm and the somnolence of the sun on my back left me lying there unmoving as he approached. I was well enough covered —bra still on, face down on the ground. He lowered himself to sit on the flat, smooth slab of bog oak embedded into the bank on the opposite side of the stream, and I lifted my head in momentary acknowledgement. He, too, stripped off his t-shirt, rinsed it in the gurgling stream, and threw it down to lay spread next to mine, one sleeve of his draped across the chest of mine, like lovers on a beach. He stayed sitting across the stream, out of reach, but now and then I would look up from the water, and our eyes would meet, before I would dip my face back down to watch the fish. We said little; we were as comfortable in our silences as we were in our conversation, and despite not talking to each other, we said so much.

"I can't be bothered to move," I told him, wordlessly, silently, with a glance and a wave of my hand. *"Let's lie here a while."*

He lay back onto the grass, face to the sun, and together, apart, we lay companionably for a while.

Suddenly, he leapt up, causing the fish to dive for cover or swish themselves away as far and fast as their fins could flap, and I recognised in him the flash of a new idea.

"Mm-hmm?" I didn't look up. Too hot, too lazy, I lay my

head down on the grass, and, with fingers still hanging over the bank into the stream, I dozed for a while, trying to ignore the sounds of whatever it was he was doing around me. First, the soft footfall of receding boots. Next, a thump of something heavy onto the soft grass, not close enough to make me startle or worry. A swoosh of water—the water trough then; he must be cleaning it out. I opened an eye, and, sure enough, in the gateway of the next field, the old bath lay on its side, its contents already seeping into the dry ground. Strange, I thought, to do it now; that field was long empty of livestock, and as the gate stood open to allow access to the stream, the trough was redundant anyway. I closed my eyes again, and when I woke up, the bath lay empty, forlorn on the patch of bare mud in the shade of the budding trees, like a shipwreck marooned on a dry beach. Charles was gone, and my vest top was dry.

The next day, the early heatwave was still in full force. Dandelions lay across the fields, as if a thousand mini suns had splintered away, too much for April to bear, and lay discarded on the grass. As I drove into the yard, the day was already warm, and the promise of another fine day hung in the sky where the clouds should have been. Charles was nowhere to be seen, in the house or out. I sent him my usual shorthand for "I'm here; where are you, and what're you up to?" in a text that simply read, *Charles?*

Stream—his answer equally economic. As I said, we didn't need many words.

Okay, office work first x Sometimes it was easier to get on with the paperwork when he was too far away to distract me, although, by now, he could distract my thoughts however far or near he may be. I dragged a small table outside and sat in the early morning sun to drink tea and balance books and edit articles. Already, the summer calendar was filling fast, and the sun's brightness was reflected into the schedule. Our business was beginning to shine.

When enough paperwork was done to allow the beginnings of boredom to seep in, I called him.

"You coming up for coffee, or will I come and find you?"

Coffee, this time, won out, and by the time I'd packed away the papers and re-boiled the kettle, I could hear the Jeep on the gravel as he swung into the yard. By now, we were at the 'greeting-with-a-kiss' stage, but our hug that morning was brief, interrupted by the sound of a second vehicle approaching. We sprung apart, rabbits almost caught in headlights, but with enough bounce to move fast enough to avoid capture. As one of our staff arrived, I resigned myself to adding a third cup to the tray and focusing on more work.

"Where'd you go yesterday?" I asked before Maria got close enough to come between us.

"Show you later," he said, with a look that added silently, *"when it's just us."* We held each other's gaze for a little too long, my yearning mirrored in his eyes.

As Maria parked and joined us, I passed him his coffee, our fingers brushing a promise between us that left me desperate to shake Maria off.

With the Easter weekend looming, we had three cabins to prepare, and the rest of the morning was taken with the safe division of tackling one each. Charles was always more cautious, and when I had suggested I video him working on the first one while Maria organised the welcome packages, his fear of being caught insisted we do it his way this morning, giving me an impatient hour of bed making, cabin tidying, and furniture straightening to do alone with my thoughts. When I look back now, I can only presume that we were not as subtle as we thought and that our most regular staff had recognised our secret even before we acknowledged it to ourselves—long before we made it a secret we needed to keep. As much as I enjoyed the company of all our team, they must surely have realised I was forever looking to set them jobs that left Charles and I together, whilst they worked elsewhere.

With the cabins done, Maria and I companionably organised the welcome packs, which I then photographed in situ on the cabin tables, whilst Charles made lunch for us all. Finally, finally, after a lazy, lingering lunch on the porch, Maria headed to the cabins in the Jeep to collect something she'd left behind. Charles and I had a moment to drown in each other's arms. We kissed, and we kissed, and we kissed, as if this moment was all we had, and then, finally, Maria's few hours of work were done. The last couple of hours of the day were our own, before Isobel would come to reclaim her home and her husband and I must return to my own.

"Come here," he said. "I've something to show you." He led me to the Jeep, and we bounced off over the fields.

"I had an idea for the campers."

As he swung the Jeep over the fields, I gripped the roof handle with one hand, to still myself against the uneven ground. My other hand, though, pressed firmly over his hand, which, in turn, rested on my leg. Although it was only my leg he held, I felt the touch ripple in waves of expectation in ever-increasing patterns throughout the rest of my body, and every now and then, he turned from watching where he was driving to smile at me. I miss his eyes most of all, I think. I miss the way we looked into each other's eyes and saw ourselves looking back.

As we neared the stream, a thin tangle of smoke wove a pretty trail into the clear, blue sky. Before there was time to worry about a forest fire, or a blaze of gorse, there, propped onto a wooden cradle, and nestled under the willow trees that made a border between stream and forest, was the bathtub. Under it, lay a newly dug firepit, glowing with embers and puffing a wispy smoke signal. Charles jerked the Jeep to a stop and jumped out. Even as he was rummaging in the back, the keys were still tinkling in the ignition where the lingering movement of the journey was gently swaying them back and forth.

Without waiting, I rushed to the bath, the aroma of woodsmoke and burning turf giving a flash of childhood summers of camping by babbling streams. I instantly understood his idea: a fire-heated, outdoor bath for the cabin users to relax in under the stars. Perfect. Absolutely perfect.

"It will need a screen, and maybe a bench. We could do one for each cabin, and make them totally private. You're brilliant!" I turned to throw my arms around him, and there he was beside me, a bottle of wine and two wine glasses clustered in one hand, and a couple of towels over his arm.

"Do you want to test it?" He pulled me towards him by the belt of my jeans.

We were chaste, still, and stripped only to underwear— keeping it professional, we rationalized. The water was warm, the sun warmer. The guilt of wine in the afternoon, hotter still, yet the rest, just right. Absolutely perfect. I reclined in his arms and gazed across the vast stretch of open fields in the mid-afternoon sun. The whole world was our own, the water was just the right temperature, and, although it was only afternoon, and far from dark, it felt as if absolutely nothing stood between us and our sunset.

I nudge the hot tap with my foot, to top up the cooling bathwater. I am not ready to get out and face the reality of James, and my children, or the cold water I am desperately trying to stay afloat in.

CHAPTER TWENTY-SIX

ESSENTIAL

*E*veryone deserves a little trip into fantasy land from time to time, and when *real* is too hard, fantasy offers me respite. So, I made a princess and a prince, a wizard, and a fairy from my clay. For good measure and commercial hope, I also made three more snowmen and another Mary and Joseph. Someone bought a Mary a few weeks ago, but not a Joseph. Maybe they thought Mary was just as well to hang on their Christmas tree without a man by her side. She can hold her precious baby forever alone, or possibly surrounded by other decorations—baubles and sparkle and glitter—and enjoy the magical mixture of serenity and excitement only a Christmas tree can bring. She'll have plenty of time to think, hanging there alone, mesmerized by a rhythmic beat of Christmas tree lights, flashing in time to choirs singing carols in high-pitched voices, proclaiming peace on Earth and goodwill to all mankind.

I am feeling short of goodwill to men today, although my goodwill to others has been exercised this morning in my annual effort at charity and helping those less fortunate and all that. I am helping a local team collect hundreds of gift-laden shoeboxes to send to war-torn Europe. This is the surest way to bring on an equal division of Christmas spirit and Christmas irritation directed at other people's inadequacies. I should take this moment to think about how well off I really am, and that, although my life is in disarray, I am not being shot at.

Oh, hang on a minute; I might be yet. Isobel calls while I am standing in a school playground, surrounded by happy children bearing brightly wrapped shoeboxes, huge smiles, and a large helping of Christmas kindness. Isobel is home and cannot wait to talk to me. For a minute, it feels like before, when we were friends, until I hear what she is calling to say.

Dear Isobel,

It was good of you to phone to let me know you are home. I am impressed you translated my 'sorry our friend is dead' message to your husband to actually mean 'please get in bed with me, since your wife is away.' Is that the American/English language divide?—a bit like the tomAYto/tomAHto thing we also debated sometimes? I also appreciate how threatened you feel by my child spending 30 minutes a week in the company of your children while they have their French lesson, and that you feel that stopping this immediately will restore all order to your home and family. I will tell my daughter an appropriate lie to explain this to her, and I assume you will pick your own lie to tell your daughters. Please thank them for their allowing my daughter to share their teacher, and their time. Please thank them too for spending four years being like sisters to my children. I hope your children are not as upset at your decision as my daughter will be. I understand you feel 'only essential contact' may now be permitted between our families. I assume you will determine what is essential. I

assume if you need to say something, it will be considered essential, but if I have something to say, it will not be? It is very considerate of you to take such complete control of Charles, and I am sure he is grateful for no longer having to think for himself or make any decisions whatsoever. But, yes, I agree, I too am glad we had a calm and civil conversation. Despite your disbelief, I really do wish you well, for although I know I have, I really never meant to hurt you. I just wish you could understand how much he hurt me too . . .

Almost as soon as Isobel and I finish our conversation, before I can even finish composing my answers in my head, I receive a text from Charles, and my chest aches as I stand in the cold playground, trying not to swear at the cluster of excited children who will not back off and leave me to my phone calls. Later, once I am home and my time is my own to wallow in, I realise James has also received a message from Charles. I type out a response.

Dear Charles,

Thank you for your text demanding only essential contact from now on, and for making sure James received a copy of that message too. I must just ask you whether that was actually essential *contact, since Isobel had told me the same message on the phone approximately two minutes before you sent the text, within your earshot . . .*

~

Dear Charles,

James is contemplating some 'essential contact' with you, involving his borrowing a shotgun from someone . . .

I never thought I would come to hate him, but now I think the day is coming very, very close …

Dear Charles,

How is it that you seem to have forgotten that you share the blame in this? Who are you to tell James to leave your family alone?

And suddenly, I realise I cannot defend Charles anymore.

CHAPTER TWENTY-SEVEN

PRINCES AND PRINCESSES

*S*omething strange happened in the kiln-firing this time around. I was pleased, after the first, *bisque*, firing, with my prince and princess, gnome, wizard and elf. Despite being unnecessary to the commercial assets of my market stall, they were made for a creative break from the tedium of angels. I liked the way they came out. Even once I'd applied the underglaze, they still looked good, and I was pleased. So, it was with an impressive degree of optimism that I applied the coats of gloss glaze and sent them for their final firing.

It was James who noticed my prince no longer looked as I had thought he should. The gold on his crown had run, obscuring his face, and destroying his looks. He was, in my eyes, a handsome and desirable fellow, and the princess thought she needed him to complete her. I had planned to sell them as a set, and as a happy ending from any storybook. She is tall and pink and proud and beautiful, and now she must stand alone. He, however, is to be relegated to a box of mistakes, to be discarded and eventually forgotten or thrown away. He is not what I hoped he would be.

Although the prince's face is no longer recognizable and his clothing has become disguised, the frog I painted at the base of cloak remains undamaged. All I can see of my prince is the frog he has become. How easily I slip into the realm of a children's story. At least there, I should be more likely to find a happy ending and fun; sunshine and blue skies, with fluffy clouds, talking bunny rabbits, fairies, rainbows, and only good things that sparkle. In a story, even the frog would turn out to be loved.

My accidental new career path is coming at me right from the pages of a children's picture book; I am becoming a button maker. In the picture book version of my life, this is surely a role best suited to an elderly spinster, with a lacy nightdress and small metal framed glasses on the end of her nose. Her hair is as white as the fluffy clouds in the skies of the pictures and tied up in a bun. Although she is old, and as wrinkled as a crumpled paper bag, she is clearly still beautiful. Her beauty shines from within, for she is the star character in her picture book and is happy as she stitches and toils by candlelight. I only stitch once the buttons are made, but the elderly widow stitches in her spare time too, for although she is the button maker, she has elves to help her and is not exhausted from firing her kiln twice weekly and single-handedly. Her worktable is tidy, with pretty pots of pretty paints, and pretty trays of pretty stamps, and beautiful old pieces of lace. Her lighting is always easy for her to work by, for the sun shines prettily in through her sparkling windows. And her windows sparkle because fairies clean them with feather dusters and fairy dust, not, like mine, only see-through once a year after a vicious bout of temper-cleaning. She is organised, with neat, wooden baskets displayed in orderly rows of colour-coordinated buttons, in an ascending scale of size, with even edges and matching motifs.

Her buttons look handmade and elegant. Mine, so far, are handmade and rustic.

Rustic meaning they are not even, not matching, not neat around the edges, and not all with holes large enough to daintily stitch onto blue and white-striped nightshirts to wear to bed with a nightcap and a candle. Some of mine don't emerge from my kiln with holes big enough to stitch to anything, which limits their use as actual working buttons.

Nonetheless, I am learning, and I am *in demand*. I can only guess the recession dictates that every woman in Ireland has now remembered how to knit, and that they also then deduce that because they are *making it themselves*—whatever 'it' may be—they are saving money. Twelve balls of chunky knitting wool at six euro each; one pattern at €7.99; a pair of knitting needles in the exact right size, and then—my *coup-de-grace*—the handmade buttons to finish it off. A bargain. A whole child's cardigan for only ninety euro or so. They'll have it outgrown by summer, then we can unravel it all and begin again with gloves and a hat for the next winter. Then where will my buttons be?

My buttons are popular because they are handmade, different, unique, available, and, most importantly, cheap. These people who buy them faster than I can make them will be sorry they have told me I should raise the prices, for this week, I have raised the prices. I was selling buttons for a paltry one euro each—and handmade and individual at that. People bought them and told their friends and put in special request orders. I race against time every week to make what they ask for, despite needing approximately seven million buttons to fill the kiln to economic firing capacity instead of two-buttons-on-an-empty-shelf capacity. People buy them and tell me I have a new career and there is demand and I could sell them to shops and everywhere, and I look on the internet to see if they are right. I see they are, for I found the equivalent of my one-euro buttons are selling for fifteen, twenty euro. For *one* button! I acknowledge that, in some cases, their creators have signed these buttons, but, hey, I can sign my buttons, if it makes for an extra fourteen euro on the price tag. Just watch me sign them. So, this week, I will raise my prices. I now have a range that vary from one euro to two fifty, and some are even stitched onto off-cuts of ancient gingham cotton scraps and are priced as a set for . . . ooh, a total of three whole euro *and* fifty cents. I will become as content and calm as the spinster button-making lady in the storybook, as I bask in the wealth accumulating from selling my buttons. I will soon be rich enough for a holiday in the sun.

It is only three weeks now until my holiday in England. This will not be a holiday in the sun, but it will be a holiday —'a change as good as a rest'—and a time to hold my family together for a while. Christmas is nearly here, but the elves are not helping me much this year. Since the old lady in the storybook is doing so well, perhaps she'd share her elves. But I have noticed lately that sharing is not what some people do, and in the blink of a text message, my pages have been turned once more, and the descent into murder mystery seems more inevitable by the moment.

Except there would only be murder and not really much mystery.

For today, I am spitting blood, raging, and shaking with anger all over again at the latest dagger Charles has put in my back. I was trying so hard to reinvent myself as a button maker, and he has reminded me once again of what I am not.

CHAPTER TWENTY-EIGHT

THURSDAY

*I*t started, as it did in another lifetime, with civility and niceness—which, of course, took me so much by surprise I didn't know what to do with it. His text began with *Hi*, which I immediately had issues with, for "Hi" is surely a greeting of familiarity. It is for someone you know or speak to on regular occasions or know well enough that even after two months of silence, you will instantly know this is a message from a friend. "Hi" is a greeting for a friend or, at least, a close acquaintance. "Hi" is not for a stranger or from a stranger or a formal conversation with someone you once did business with. It is not a greeting from someone you don't know.

He was informing me that our accounts are finalised, and we must meet with our accountant. He suggested Thursday would suit our accountant but politely and considerately acknowledged that Thursday may not suit me, since I now have another life he has chosen to distance himself so far from he can no longer be certain of how I spend my Thursdays. And he suggests that if Thursday does not suit me, another day may instead. ***Or next week,*** his text suggests, will do fine if I am busy on Thursday.

I am busy when his text arrives, and my hands are covered with clay. I cannot decide how to answer, so I do not wash the clay from my hands but simply carry on with what I am busy doing, and I do not answer.

The clay is not quite distraction enough to stop me from composing a thousand answers in my head, but it is distraction enough to stop me sending them. James questions whether this message from Charles is 'essential contact.' It is, of course, but I realise I am now scared to reply, because I am scared to see him again. I am particularly scared I will become emotional or overwhelmed or that the meeting will not be as I planned it in my head: he has no car in the daytime, so I will pick him up to drive us to the accountant; we will sit in silence, as I am unsure of what to say anymore and will not want to risk a fight. No, we will not sit in silence; we will make polite conversation and ask about the children. Or we will definitely sit in silence, for even to ask about the children will make me feel like crying, and I must not cry, not anymore, while he is watching me. We will meet with the accountant, and I will drive us to the bank, and we will close the account, and I will suggest we get coffee in the hotel in the small town where our bank is, and we will have a chance to say, "Nice knowing you, I miss you, sorry, goodbye." Please, if nothing else, give me a chance to say goodbye.

But, of course, we will not. He will refuse my offer of a lift in my car, and I will suggest that since he will be borrowing his mother's car and driving past my house, he should pick me up, and he will drive me to the accountant. We will sit in silence or discuss the weather or the weekend's sports results. But he will not pick me up; he will not allow himself—or be allowed—to stop near my house and be seen with me in his company. Although our affair is long over and our friendship is dead and I no longer even know this man, he will not be allowed to share car space while we travel from the same village to the same place to close a business we built together.

So, we will travel ridiculously, separately, independently, and individually, probably one behind the other, indicating simultaneously as, once again, we travel the exact same path. We will barely acknowledge each other but greet our accountant with friendly warmth while sitting in hostility beside each other, side by side, inches apart, but with a gulf the size of America between us.

Then we will leave the accountant and travel separately to close the bank account, and there will be no coffee, and, once again, no goodbye. And I know that I cannot do it his way without danger of emotion and anger and upset and tears. I probably can't do it my way without any of these either, so I continue to roll clay, and do not answer his text. I also do not answer it the next day, and I wonder if he will contact me again to ask me again when it suits me to meet.

So, I do not say I will rearrange my Thursday to suit him, as I would have done in our old lifetime, and I do not offer to collect him, or ask him to collect me, and I do not offer a list of alternative dates next week that would suit me instead, and I do not try to chat. Above all else, I certainly do not say, "Hi," because the last time I offered friendship in the wake of the death of our friend, our children paid the price in the cessation of their French classes and their only remaining time together.

In the end, on Wednesday evening, I settle simply for *I am busy tomorrow,* and I expect him to reply with a repeat of *When it suits you* but I hear nothing. And on Thursday morning, I still hear nothing.

I have made a decision in the market, which is proving to be stressful, and my relaxing, head-freeing, calming time in the market is becoming difficult and causing me to have to think and make choices. I have struggled to be certain in the choices I have made, but now I have made the choice and so, on that particular Thursday, I am following it through. James and I are building a table and shelving to fill the new, bigger space I have committed to.

I am happy to take on a bigger space, because I want to fill a bigger space and have more room to display both my own wares—particularly my rapidly expanding button range —but, also, sadly, to keep shifting the surplus stock that Santa should have, throughout weekends in December, been distributing to the children visiting him at the Cabin in the Woods Christmas extravaganza, if they have been good enough this year. But since I have not been good enough this year, Santa will not come, and I am left with boxes of carefully crafted gifts that Santa will give to no one. Bulk buying in the summer for economy and certainty in our future means hundreds of beautiful wooden toys, reminiscent of traditional childhood, are left over. They were among the detritus that Isobel packaged up when she dumped the rest of my life back onto my own doorstep. These Christmas toys, abandoned and unwanted, remind me again that for us, at least, childhood is over. Nonetheless, the wooden toys are popular on my stall amongst my clay, and I will sell what I can. I need the money to feed my family and pay the bills, and so a larger stall is a good move. The cost, however, of taking on a bigger space is the loss of the brightness and open outlook from my table next to the café, the soundtrack from the speaker directly over my head pounding its steady beat of nostalgic Christmas clichés. I will miss the stallholders who have become my neighbours and made me smile and bought me coffee. I will be unanchored once more, unsignposted, without the ability to say, "I am next to the café" so my increasing clientele of button shoppers could easily locate me.

Even greater than all this that I will lose, is the loss of my own space behind my own table, with my own rules and my own display and my own time keeping and only myself to Hoover for. My new, bigger space will be shared, and I am more nervous now of sharing than of any other sacrifice. I shared before, and now I am the child who shared her favourite toy and got it back used and broken. I may not know how to share again. I will sacrifice my bright table, my aroma of fresh coffee, and my banter with Computer-fixing Man, but I am scared to share my space and my conversation and my thinking time.

Still, I allow myself to give in to excitement, and I am pleased to be able to build a bigger space. I have planned it out in my head, and I will have a whole wall of buttons and a dedicated button-browsing shelf. I will enjoy decorating and dressing the space, and I will be happy to have more room and more potential. I will be happy that James and I are driving to the market together to build me a temporary future, and we will have something to talk about and plans to make and wood to buy and a day ahead together with a real focus.

It is as we are driving towards the market, when I get the call from the accountant. He tells me that he has just met with Charles, who called him at ten o'clock that morning to say he was on his way to meet, and now all the accounts are finalised, and I must go in and sign the cheques Charles has left with him for my attention, and suddenly, I am nothing but rage. Charles has destroyed my day with James in a single moment.

It is suddenly apparent that the text he sent in the week to say, **'Hi'** and **'When it suits you'**, was not, in fact, 'essential contact' after all, and I was right to disbelieve the fleeting glimpse I had of the Charles I used to know. All I can do is tear shreds off our accountant and berate him for dealing with my business behind my back, without me and without informing me this meeting was going ahead. In response, all he could say was that he, too, had expected me to be there, and Charles simply told him I couldn't make it. I must go in next week so our accountant can tell me the same things he has told Charles and so I can sign the same cheques Charles has signed. And, of course, although it is unreasonable of me to be angry with the accountant, he must be secretly delighted. He is a man who bills by the hour and must now have two separate meetings with us instead of one. Once again, Charles is costing me money I no longer have, and I am raging and raging and raging.

Without conscious thought, and even though James is sitting beside me, in the driving seat, listening to his day with me and my future drain away, I hit the buttons to dial Charles. When he answers, I am incoherent, and the tears are threatening to get in my way again. I can only say, "How dare you? How *dare* you? You sent me a text that said, *'Hi,'* and you asked me when it suits me." And then I am so angry I cannot even speak, and so I hang up.

Our accountant told me that since Charles is a local man and our bank is a local bank, and this is smalltown, rural Ireland, it is very possible that he could close our account without my signature. It has only been a couple weeks since I went into the bank and set it so we both must sign to close the account, but now I am worried the accountant is right. I worry that Charles may do exactly what I have tried to stop, and so I wonder if I can do it first. I think I am not callous and manipulative, although I know I am sometimes seen to be exactly that, but, on this Thursday, I must become exactly those things. Charles is holding all the bank details, and I do not even know the account number. I am not known in the bank, because I am just a blow-in girl with an English accent who has not been using this bank for a lifetime, and whose granny never stepped foot through the bank doors. Because of all these things, I must get the paperwork from him however the hell I can, and as fast as possible.

But when I text him to bring the paperwork to my house in case I have questions when I meet with the accountant, he says he will not. I assure him that I am not home, and no one is at my home today, and please leave it there for me, but he still says he will not. Stubborn, ridiculous, laughable—if only I could laugh—he agrees to leave it with the accountant whom he has, only a short while ago, taken it from. So once again, he drives in a borrowed car right past my house, which is only two minutes' drive from his own, to our accountant's office, which is ten miles away, and this, he thinks, is sensible, rational, and reasonable. Although I stop in my raging to think how lucky he is to not be considering the price of unnecessary petrol, I remember that it is, of course, his elderly mother's car, and the petrol will be paid for on her pension and not from his pocket. I used to be amazed that he would take her petrol without recompense, and even more so that he would often borrow my car and return it with the petrol light on, but now . . . now I am no longer surprised that he could take anything from anyone.

So, James and I build my space in the market, and I try to quash my rage, to regain the day James and I had intended. First, though, I allow my anger to rise as stupidity and send one final text to Charles. I know he and Isobel will feel this is non-essential contact, but he still brings out the child in me, and today, I am the four-year-old with the temper tantrum, and now . . . now I know our accountant has my bank details, I don't need to feign politeness or cling to friendship anymore. My final text of the day is to tell Charles he is pathetic and that I hope one day someone treats him the way he treats others. Despite the level of communication we have sustained through the day, and the first 'conversation' we have had in weeks, it is no surprise that he does not reply to this last text. I wonder this time if he even shared today's conversation with Isobel, for if I were him, I would be too ashamed to let her know how ridiculous he is being. I don't know whether she is either unaware of the 'non-essentialness' of this series of texts that he started with *Hi* earlier in the week, or if she agrees with me enough to remain quiet this time. Whatever the reason, even Isobel has not chastised me for this day's loss of temper.

After all this, James and I do not achieve as much in the market as we had hoped. The combination of shaking with rage and shaking with cold leaves the air between us as frosty as the air around us. It is so cold in the market that the paint on my button sign will not dry, and before we have agreed which way around to place the table, it is time to collect our children, and our day is left in tatters.

CHAPTER TWENTY-NINE

REVENGE OF THE NINJA GIRL

*I*t is raining again. I am alone in the house, putting off a stack of housework that is higher than I can reach today, but the kitchen is warm, so I will make more clay instead. My daughter is beginning to be old enough to think she doesn't need me. November has given way to December, and her class has gone on a school trip to Dublin for a carol concert. She will not be home till midnight. She cried when I brushed her hair and would not let me walk her to the bus once she noticed her friends' mothers had not got out of their cars. And it seems that perhaps Charles was right indeed to feel threatened by my nine-year-old, as, whilst waiting for the bus to arrive, she carefully crossed the road and dropped two important envelopes into the post box on the pub wall.

One is her letter to Santa to let him know we will be away for Christmas, and that she would like a treat for her pony and something nice for Jess, and not to worry if he can't afford to bring her much this year but thanks all the same for last year's presents. If I were Santa, her letter would fill me with a warm, snugly glow, like the children on the old Ready Brek adverts always seemed to have. I would fill her stocking with the most amazing things she would adore, although she didn't know she wanted them until she unwrapped them. So, I hope the letter, addressed to 'Santa, c/o the Post Office, or at the North Pole', finds a safe landing place in the hearts of those who watch over her.

The second envelope contains not a letter, but a storyboard. She has, with no prompting or encouragement from me, planned revenge. She has given in to despair and acknowledgment of the reality of having her contact severed and her French lessons cancelled. Her friendships and her nearly-sisterhood relations with Charles's children are already becoming a painful and blurring memory. To deal with this, she has come up with a plan.

Her storyboard clearly and amusingly—amusing to me, but probably not to its recipient—illustrates a karate attack. She has been taking karate lessons for around a year, and suddenly, I wish I was taking them too. I also have a sudden realisation these lessons fall very securely into the category of Money Well Spent.

Picture one on the storyboard depicts *The Arrival*. One of Charles's nieces, with whom we have maintained friendship and closeness, has kindly collected my karate-girl daughter, and chauffeured her to the doorstep of Charles's house. In this picture, she's donning the karate suit, the black belt is fastened with authority and confidence, and the ninja mask, for disguise, is over my little ninja's head. The driver will not be in disguise since the car will be recognizable anyway. This will, my daughter asserts, lull Charles into the false security that his visitor is both friendly and family.

By picture two, Ninja-girl is sneaking into the kitchen of the farmhouse, and the picture depicts a tiptoeing stance that leaves the viewer in no doubt as to the quiet and the suspense.

The build-up would be incredible, if only he knew, but the Charles in this storyboard is blissfully unaware of his attacker's approach.

Picture three—there he is! How I wish I were there to watch. I should retrieve the envelope from the post box, and slice it open, so I can draw myself into the picture with my nose pressed against the window in a prime position for a perfect view. He will not be able to help but recognise himself in these pictures, for he is, as always—even in the house—wearing a cap. It must be him, and he must realise it. I wonder if he is still looking at the storyboard and understanding her evil plan, or if he realised instantly where it had come from, and, as with every other remnant of me that I ever wrote down, instantly destroyed it in the range. Everything I ever wrote him, fuel for his range to keep himself warm. He is—in my daughter's picture, but probably also in reality at the time the post arrives . . . I cannot forget how well I know his day—leaning against the sink, waiting for the kettle to boil. Does he remember now to put in less water, as he no longer has to make enough tea to share with me at this time of day? Perhaps he already makes tea for someone else. Perhaps Isobel drives home from work around this time each day, to share his tea and ensure no one else does.

By picture four, the ninja has struck. I am shocked and amused that my nine-year-old has actually written the word, *'Balls'* on her storyboard—*The Ninga* [she spells, nine-year-old-ishly] *Kicks him in the Balls.* I was too busy trying not to laugh to point out that I have learned he has no balls, and her secret assassin self will have to kick him several times while she is trying to find them. In the picture, it is all over with one swift kick, and the next picture shows him doubled over on the floor. I hope he is in tears of pain, hurt, humility, love, and loss. The pictures have, in a rare reason for laughter, left me in tears of hilarity. This, at least, is a win. Meanwhile, Ninja-girl sneaks swiftly out the door and into the waiting getaway car, which the niece has turned and has waiting with the engine running.

Picture six, of course, shows nothing but smoke and dust. The car has left in a cloud of it, and Charles is, no doubt, engulfed in the steaming of his rage. I am shocked that I have allowed her to post it, but he had promised her he would talk to her, let her ask him why, and let her say goodbye. In doing none of these things, she has begun to hate him too. I think she is justified in posting an anonymous threatening letter, and he is lucky she hasn't laced the envelope with a hefty dose of anthrax. Isobel will probably fulfil her promise to report us for assault if I 'attacked' him again; this nine-year-old's attack is a far more real threat to his dignity than the smack in the face I gave him.

My heart aches for this child who had this friend who carried her on his shoulders and pushed her on the swing and shared his farm and his forest and his children with her. He welcomed her into his house as one of his own children, and she stayed on overnights, both on necessary occasions when James and I were away, and also on unnecessary occasions when I was working late or she was having fun playing in the house or we had stayed up drinking and the children had fallen asleep and we simply left them safe and warm, sprawled across sofas or in his children's beds, promising to collect in the morning in time for coffee. I wish he would understand how much he has taken from this child who loved him so much.

I wonder what lies or truths he has given to his own children who I, and my family, all loved so much. I think of his children and miss them still and often. Even now, although he would never protect mine from anything anymore, despite having carried my daughter on his shoulders only three—how can it possibly be only three when it feels like a lifetime ago?—months ago, I will still and always do my best for his children.

And that is why I have, once more, made uninvited contact with both him and with Isobel.

As I play around with the glazes and clay and coloured slips salvaged from the one pottery workshop we had launched in the summer with a promise that it would be the start of many, my experimenting becomes both more extreme and more confident. As I try more and more, and more again, techniques and styles and forms with clay, I also am doing more and more and more damage to my lungs. On every occasion I forget to wear a mask, the dust and the fumes and the ground-up liquid glass that the glazes are made from burn into my lungs and leave me gasping for air. And one box of glaze is still unaccounted for, and I only remember where it was in the lifetime I lived so long ago but only three months ago. And so, I must send a message to warn him that these glazes are dangerous and that if they are still at the farm, he must make sure to keep his children safe. I will, still and always, try to keep the children safe. I know they have been told I have wrecked their world, but I have not done it alone, and I care about them still. One day, I hope I can tell them this.

I hear nothing from Charles. I cannot tell whether he reads any text I send him now, or whether he sees my name in his inbox and deletes me, over and over again, and if deleting me is now an unconscious and automatic response for him and he does not even realise he has done it. I wonder if he will go out and find the missing glazes and actually force his daughters to drink, inhale, and smear them around their skin, just to spite me further. I wonder whether he cares at all.

Isobel though … Isobel must sense in me the mother who is appealing to the mother she is, hoping to offer belated but necessary protection for something I can still protect them from. She acknowledges with thanks, with conversation, and with a request to let her know if I think of anywhere else she must look. She thanks me, and we communicate with a glimmer of the friendship that used to exist. I am suddenly certain that one day we will meet, and we will talk. I am relieved and grateful that she has acknowledged that while I cannot change the past, I still care enough for her and her children to protect from danger where I must.

I still have Charles named as the emergency contact for my daughter on her school details, and I must change the records to correct this. I know I need to, but I cannot bring myself to enter the school and say, "If my child is sick or bleeding, or has broken limbs or another childhood crisis, and if, at that single and unexpected moment where she needs me and I am not contactable, if, if you can't get hold of me, or of James, and then you phone Charles to say, 'Come, please come, this child needs you,' he would refuse to come."

I cannot tell the school this, because I still can't tell myself this, although I know it is true. I hope the make-believe girl in the ninja suit gets to him and haunts his dreams.

But I hope Isobel sees the funny side of the storyboard and laughs and laughs.

CHAPTER THIRTY

PETTY CASH

*I*n the envelope along with the threat of the ninja
attack storyboard, I enclosed a very short (and
unsigned—but who else would it be?) note to explain this had
nothing to do with me, but I think she is justified in sending
it. I also scribbled a brief warning, a PS to my note: *Watch
out for ninja attacks, especially on your birthday.* His
birthday is today, and the day the storyboard will arrive in his
post box—I don't want him to think I had forgotten his
birthday. I have had no response. I have had no contact for
days. I guess I am not essential anymore.

I have been unsuccessful in emptying our joint bank
account myself, but I feel a relative triumph in the discovery
that he has not done so either, and will not be able to. It seems
my efforts to ensure joint signatures during the week of The
Slap have either served to protect me now, or thwarted my
own possibilities in taking it all for my own. I do, of course,
believe I have earned it all; he has doubled our accountant
fees by meeting without me, he has doubled them again
submitting unbalanced books and incomplete records, and he

also has the entire contents of the cashbox. And the actual cashbox. Which was mine all along. I would quite like my cashbox back, in fact. It is a bit of a struggle to multi-task these days in the form of simultaneously being in the market and at craft fairs. I have to work from a margarine tub at the craft fairs, so it is no wonder I am not making a huge profit when the image I am presenting is not one of a business-like cashbox owner. I would like to leave the margarine tub at the market with my son, who, now the school holidays are here and exams and cramming are over, is babysitting my stall for me. But, despite the potential for hiding the un-business-like margarine tub behind the drapes of the tablecloths, my son flatly refuses to lower the fantastically high standard I have created for my market stall and fights me for the real cashbox on threat of not minding the stall. So I get the margarine tub. And I pack a carload of wares and take myself to a local craft fair. I pitch up under another speaker blaring another endless loop of nostalgia, broken momentarily only by screeching feedback when the local celebrity steps up to declare the fair open. It is a slow day for me, as the money is spent on cheap e-numbers and games with ugly teddies as prizes. I barely need to expose the margarine tub, and I do little to fill it with cash, but I am rewarded for my time nonetheless by winning first prize in the raffle, and the mixture of cheap wine and huge chocolate boxes consoles me well enough for my two-hour stint behind a small table in a noisy village hall full of running children and a squeaky microphone.

I cannot ask Charles for the cashbox back, for it will be perceived not only as non-essential contact (how can they know whether it is essential to me or not to have my cashbox returned? How can they be certain I have not suddenly a great excess of cash in need of a small red cashbox? How can they be certain all I now own in terms of money would not fit with room to spare into the small red cashbox and I have no real need for the bigger blue one I pretend to fill each weekend?) but also as an unwelcome reminder of the smack-in-the-face day. Assault? No way!

Either he still knows me better than I allowed credit for, or there has been a great moment of coincidence. He either anticipated my threat of attack would involve a visit to the bank, or he received our final statement in the post, along with the ninja warning, because I have received a text from him. There is no *"Hi"* in this morning's text, so he has learned something at least, but a more formal ***Morning*** and a notification that our final cheques are cleared and—get this— he asks, ***When it suits you,*** to close the account. We've been here before with the 'when it suits me' question, and this time, I will be nicer—little nicer, anyway. I am still short in my reply, but it is instant and suggests we must meet to close the account or it becomes infinitely more complicated, and I tell him I was in the bank myself yesterday and have the form. He asks if we can simply go in and close the account and withdraw the money there and then. This thwarts me, and I must admit to him that I don't know. Once the banker told me that my measures to ensure Charles could not empty the account himself are firm enough to ensure I also cannot close it alone, I left with only a phone number of a faceless Galway based name who "deals with your business account." This faceless person will advise me on how to close the account without possibility of meeting with my co-signer face to face. I need them to tell me how to also avoid giving him my signature on a form, and thus allowing him to draw the money for himself. However, Charles surprises me, by easily agreeing to meet. Maybe he is also in a desperate enough financial place that he, too, needs eight hundred euro even more than he needs to avoid me.

When Charles agrees to meet, I explain I have only a tiny window of time. I am free this morning but have no transport. I have broken both wing mirrors on my car by getting into another tight spot—this time due to only the laziness of not opening my gates fully before driving through them on Tuesday morning. Some urgent need to see either me or my signature on our form dictates that Charles quickly volunteers to collect me. The catch, as always, comes in the form of a chaperone. When he arrives at my gate, he is in his mother's car, with his mother in it. She, it seems, rather conveniently needs to also go to the same bank at this exact time on this Thursday morning when it 'suits him', and when I have learned to make it suit me this time. I want to argue the point and suggest a time without his mother present, but I haven't the time to spare to be difficult today.

Amazingly, he assumes a concern over my life and children when I open the door to greet him and he sees my daughter is home and sick, wrapped in pyjamas and fleecy dressing gown. I leave her behind and start up the drive to meet him, unwilling to let him into my home or my life, and he asks if someone is with my daughter. James is home, sleeping after a night-shift, but I don't tell Charles this. I am disappointed he has come to think so little of me that he thinks I would leave a nine-year-old alone, but even so, what right does he have now to question this? Who is he, to pretend concern for my childcare arrangements after all that has been said and done? Although disappointed by his trust in me, I am impressed by his concern for my daughter. Still, I do not deign to answer his questions, because no part of my daughter's care is his concern any longer. Those days of involving him in my children's care are finished, by his choice, and I will not let him back in. If I let him think I am leaving her alone, maybe, just maybe, he will care. My daughter, of course, is desperate to see him and to ask if he received his 'birthday card'—aka her ninja story—but I shield them from each other. I close the door on her, and I don't speak to him.

He holds the car door open and tips the seat forward for me to climb into the back. I acknowledge his mother with a "How are you?" but still don't speak to him. I simply don't know what I should say to him. There is so much I want to say and nothing I can say, especially when his mother is with us. They chat in the front of the car, and I look out the window and pretend not to care, until she directs a question to me. For the rest of the short journey, I become unwillingly involved in a conversation about the children and exams and university choices, but I am mono-syllabic, and when he adds his questions to hers, I volunteer as little information as I can. I share a fleeting glance with Charles in the mirror, but look away immediately, to avoid accidentally exchanging any unspoken words. She asks me what university choices my son is making. Charles asks me if my son is still applying for the career path he had been planning in the summer when they discussed it together over his kitchen table and tea. I tell Charles's mother that I am a little short on cash now I'm jobless, and I don't see a way for my son to pursue the career he wants. She laughs nervously at my reply, as if I may be joking. I'm hurt by her response, but I accept it as her acknowledgement of recession and universal hardship. I am sure this lovely eighty-year-old woman who my children called 'Granny' means us no harm, and equally certain she knows nothing else about the choices Charles and I made and the outcomes they led to. But when Charles laughs too, I want to say to his mother, "Look what your son has done to my family! He has taken my income from me, and he has taken my son's educational choice and freedom! How can you not know who he really is?" I want to ask her if she is proud of what her son has done to me and my family, but I know he has told her nothing. I wonder what story he *has* told her to explain the loss of the business and the loss of me in their lives.

In the bank, things become even more strained, and the fighting begins. I'm ashamed that I cannot be nice, but I'm too stubborn in my reasoning that when I tried to be nice, he was not, and I will not be nice today just to suit his choice. I'm infuriated to realise my fear of smalltown banking is coming to fruition when the cashier greets him by name, chats about the family, and addresses each comment only to him as he goes through the motions of closing our account. By the time she has spoken only to him for the fifth time, I'm angry enough to lean across him and address her myself.

"Excuse me. This is a joint account, and I, too, am standing here." Her apologetic reply does her no favours as she informs me that she didn't know who I was. I am too shaken with the strain of standing next to him at all to question her on how, then, is she proceeding to close a joint account requiring joint signatures when she assumes I am not here at all? When she goes to file forms, I pick another fight by suggesting to Charles that he has no right to an equal half of the cash. I justify this with his refusal to meet our accountant together, and so upping our fees. Whereas before, when we first entered the bank, it was his proximity that made me shake, now it is pure rage that has me shaking as I whisper-shout that he has also assumed ownership of all the money in the cashbox.

And that is the moment, when, at a time when I'm beginning to think we've exhausted every possible cliché in the saga of our lives and our heartache, he throws in the biggest cliché of them all so far. He is adamant that it is equal halves, and that if I do not agree, he will not sign, and then, he says—I still cannot believe he actually said this—"Then you won't get your hands on it at all."

He really, truly, actually uses the words, "won't get your hands on it," in relation to our mutual cash, and, for a moment, I am torn between raging and laughing. We stand here in the bank, a foot apart but a world apart, and even as I stand there, I think once I have had a night to get over it, I will choose to laugh, because it was the funniest thing he could have said. We hold eye contact, and I realise again how much I miss looking into his eyes and reading his thoughts. This shared look in the bank contains passion for sure, but now it is a fierce passion of the hating kind, rather than the fierce passion I long to see.

"You won't get your hands on any of it!" And, as we stand there, glaring at each other, as if we truly detest each other, the fight goes from me. Eight hundred euro is not enough to change anything, but I am in a sorry enough financial state that I can't argue about it, and he knows it. I can't fight anymore, so I take my half of the cash and leave the bank, thinking that we will, at least, get a few precious minutes of conversation whilst we wait in the car for his mother to finish shopping. He doesn't follow me straight out though, and his mother is already waiting in the car. When he returns to the car a few minutes later, we drive home without words, and for the first time since we met and travelled anywhere in the same car, he doesn't meet my eyes in the rear-view mirror. I watch him for a moment and can see a real hint of something sad and broken in his eyes, but still, he won't look into mine. He won't notice the reflection of his soul as it drowns in my welling tears.

Finally, after a journey I both want to end and to last forever, we are at my gateway, and he opens the door and flips the seat to let me out. At last, he speaks, and of all the things he could choose to say to finally mark the absolute end of it all; of all the things he could choose to say to acknowledge the certainty that he need never see me again now unless he wants to; of all the thousand unspoken thoughts and words, the ones he chooses to use as we stand at my gate with his mother in the car next to us, pretending not to listen through the open door, are "Happy Christmas."

I walk away without replying. I walk away without even trying to look into his eyes. Later, I put my answer, as ever, in a text. By texting, I can get words out without crying or shouting or emotional outbursts, and I tell him,

Dear Charles,

I hope you get exactly what you deserve this Christmas.

And then, later, much later, when I realise I still do not want this to be how it ends, I write another text,

Dear Charles

It is beyond heart-breaking that I trusted you with my heart, my soul, my dreams, my children, my money, and now I would rather leave my 9-year-old daughter home alone than risk you upsetting her anymore, and we are fighting over the last 16 cents, and accusing each other of financially cheating the other one. No one who was friends like we were should let things end this way. I am leaving for

England, with my children, on Wednesday, and despite what we have become, it was nice knowing you before all this. Goodbye.

There is no reply. He could never give me the reply I want, which is an acknowledgment that he liked knowing me too, before I became what he has helped me to become. Or even to just say goodbye.

CHAPTER THIRTY-ONE

*T*here is nothing like spending Christmas in a big house, in a remote area, overlooking the sea, surrounded by people you love and who love you. There is nothing like having all the decorations hung for you, a huge games room to keep everyone busy, comfortable beds, and *en suite* bathrooms for everyone. Mine even had a jacuzzi bath. There is nothing like it at all if what a girl needs is to 'get away from it all', relax, find some headspace, and forget the world. I should be able to have long heart-to-hearts with my sister and bond with my children and nieces. We should all have fun.

What I had overlooked from this delusional idyll of my fantasies is I had invited all the family.

"Let's recreate our childhood," I'd said to my brothers, my sister, my parents. "It'll be fun."

Yeah, right.

Another thing I had not fully thought through was the eleventh-hour addition of extending the invitation—"only for the first few days, we won't have room after that"—to include our cousin Alice. It has been about fifteen years since we saw each other: A fifteen-year gap the size of the Atlantic Ocean, births of children, deaths of parents, and, more pressingly, the break-up of her marriage and the calamity of mine. She had, as promised, arrived in Dublin the week before Christmas, and we had, as expected, fallen into each other's arms at the airport and talked as if we had not spent fifteen years growing up and changing our lives. We had not burst into tears, as her arriving without her luggage overshadowed the emotional reunion. An extra two hours at the airport, her on one side of the barrier and me waiting on the other side, had simply made us tired, confused, frustrated, and amused in fluctuating combinations. I thought I couldn't find her simply because I hadn't recognised her, so I had begun to talk to strangers in case they were her. After approaching a third random stranger who looked as lost as I was feeling, and confirming that no, she was not my long-lost relative, I took the more sensible option and asked airport staff. Alice, they confirmed, had arrived. Her luggage, they added, had not. Eventually, they let her into the arrivals hall, and there she was. Instead of recognising each other by our shattered hearts, I recognised her for her lack of luggage, and the lack of fellow passengers around her.

Tired as we were, we made the most of the car journey to cram fifteen years of catch-up and marital disarray into before James and my children would share the time and our conversations would be more limited. I recognised in her my own desperate need to talk about it, and we spilled our hearts in non-stop gabble, neither of us really listening to the other but both hearing each other's heartache regardless.

We continued to talk but not really listen for the next few days. We talked as we took Jess on endless walks. We talked as we splashed through the sodden bog; we talked as we pounded the firm ground of the road, and we talked as Isobel drove past us. And even though Alice was in Isobel's position, she did not judge or chastise, and, in return, I offered her sympathy and shock that her best friend had fallen in love with her own husband. *How could she?* I murmured, but only to myself. As I lay awake at night—endlessly awake beside James. I could hear Alice, too, was lying awake on the other side of our bedroom wall. We manage to trudge through our days, one foot in front of the other until another day is over, but we cannot hurry the nights.

We left for England a few days after Alice arrived. The big adventure I had planned with my children, to prove my capability for independence and survival, had been something to look forward to. It had given my children a focus and a topic that was new and different. It had involved excitement and anticipation, and no one had cried while we had made our plans. We were to travel alone and by public transport, from Dublin to the Lake District, and it was going to be *fun*. James, committed to work, was to follow us a few days later, alone and by car. I would have a few days to tell my siblings what was happening in my life—or to not tell them. I wasn't sure yet just how much or how little I would say. I hadn't counted on Alice. My independent streak was made less independent by having another adult along for the ride, and as we jumped from one train to the next to the next, her jetlag began to tire us all. By the third train, everyone but me was sleeping, heads nodding in time to the clacking of the rails. I, increasingly bad-tempered, was left fighting to stay awake—the responsible adult to watch over them all: my children, my cousin, our baggage, and the station signs flashing past. I could not afford to get off at the wrong station or to miss being where I needed to be.

I stayed awake as we flew from Dublin to Leeds. I stayed awake as we travelled from Leeds to Manchester. I stayed awake as we switched trains at Manchester to travel to somewhere else, and then onwards from somewhere else to somewhere else ... At first, the stations were busy, urban stations, with busy, urban people, but as we travelled northwards, the busyness gave way to less busy trains, less busy stations, and less busy country folks. With each change after Manchester, the trains became smaller, ricketier, and the passengers came and went with their own stories to tell. A young woman changed from work clothes to party clothes in the aisle across from our seats. She sprayed herself liberally with a scent that made us cough and didn't make her into anyone she hadn't been already. I wanted to tell her that spraying a new scent on your body doesn't cover the person inside. At one small station, a cat got on, carried safely in a fastened basket. I envied its security and its carrier. I wished for someone to carry me, in all the ways Charles used to, and that James wanted to. The cat was carried off again; people with dogs came and went. I expected hens, imagining this most rural of trains was no different to trains of storybooks and old-fashioned journeys across exotic lands, where hens and goats and old ladies in bright scarves would travel in a heady scent of spice, foliage, and animal. I forced my drooping eyes to stay awake as I watched Alice sleeping across from me, and no hens got on.

Eventually, we arrived at our destination, met by the landlady of the house I had found for us to stay in for our family Christmas. My sister and her family, the lady told me, had already arrived. The kettle would be on, and finally, after a long day of travel and months of a journey, someone would be as pleased to see me as I was to see them.

I had spoken to my sister many times in the past few months; I didn't tell her about Charles until it wasn't about Charles anymore, but by then, she had guessed. She knew without explanation why my business had ended, and she offered me some comfort in her understanding. My sister, it turned out, knew what I was feeling. My sister, as it turned out, had lived a similar story, unbeknown to any of us.

My sister, when I had phoned her to say, "Let's have a family holiday, my business is over," had simply asked, "Was it because of Isobel? Has she finally told you to leave?" And with those words, I knew she knew. And once I realised she knew, I knew how she knew. I have learned there are people who understand and people who don't, and the ones who do are the ones who have lived the same kind of story.

By the time we meet in the Lakes, she has filled me in on her own story, which was over long ago and never to be discussed with anyone else, so I am still free to tell her more of my own without fear of hogging the conversation. She wants to hear it all.

But, once again, things don't happen as I planned. We have minutes alone, peppered between allocating beds and rooms and food and drinks or the children and the arrival of brothers and the juggling of Alice as a last-minute addition to the party. The children are difficult, but once fed, settle down to catching up with cousins and exploring the house. Our brothers are predictable: easy once fed, and then caught—but not stopped from—slinking outside for cigarettes while "You girls can clear up the kitchen, can't you?" Alice is easy, as she is part of the conversation, but I am mindful of the mirrors between our stories, and I cannot tell my sister how much I love my friend's husband when Alice no longer has a friend or a husband. I cannot dismiss my own husband so easily while Alice is still yearning for hers. I cannot be the person who her friend is while she is listening, and so I spend many hours alone in my bedroom in the attic of this enormous house, too far away from the others to hear them laughing without me.

After that first evening meal together, I have had enough of company and pretending to my brothers that I am normal. At the first opportunity, it is me who slinks off next, and I spend the rest of the evening sitting on the window seat of my attic bedroom, looking at the concrete below and thinking about just how far it would be to fall. I spend too much time contemplating whether the fall would be far enough, and eventually, I force myself from the ledge. Finally allowing exhaustion from the day and the last three months and the last two years to get the better of me, I lose myself in the jacuzzi bathtub with the whirring of its motors drowning out the family I left downstairs on the ground floor.

As the week progresses, I watch the children play with their cousins, and they, at least, are getting the Christmas I wanted. They are happy. Their laughter fills the rooms as they run around. They spend hours playing hide and seek in this enormous house, and someone always finds the person they are looking for. They teach each other snooker on the half-size table in the games room, and my brother's wife teaches them to play her guitar while others of us watch old black and white films in another corner. We play a never-ending cycle of various boardgames and snooker matches, with any mix of the children and adults, and we remind the cousins of the fierce competitiveness and bond that only family can bring. I begin to come around to the holiday as I force myself to enjoy it. Alice leaves on the same day James arrives, and suddenly, all is well, and I am remarkably pleased James is here. As my loud and rambunctious family explode around me in familiar noise and chaos, James, once again, becomes both my lighthouse and my anchor. He brings calm to the storm that my family can be, and I cling to him, as if I no longer want to drown.

I have invented a game to involve the whole family. We are all going to kill each other. It will stop us from killing each other for real as we start to fight over whose turn it is to wash up or to cook or to yell at the children to get to sleep. My brothers hog the snooker table, and smoke outside with their partners, and don't do their share of the washing up. My sister and I don't fight at all, for once, because we are united in our fight against our brothers as they drink the last of the beer and don't wash up yet again and start on the wine that my sister and I were planning to claim after the washing up was done. My new game involves us each drawing another's name from a hat, along with a murder weapon. Through the course of the next few hours, days, or as long as it takes, we will each actively attempt to kill each other by handing our named victim the named murder weapon. I, for example, must kill my brother's girlfriend by handing her the salt. If she takes it from me, she will be dead. This game results in an entire day of people trying to pass random objects to each other, and in refusing to accept anything anyone offers. Most of us find it hilarious, and it unites us in our refusals to give or take. One by one, we die, and chaos returns as we find other things to argue about, but for a while, as we offer each other plenty, but take nothing, we have the Christmas spirit I had hoped for.

Christmas itself passes well. It begins on Christmas Eve with most of us bonding over the old ritual of midnight mass. We have found a church in a nearby village where midnight mass really takes place at midnight, instead of fobbing us off with the 9 p.m. version I get at home in our small Irish village. (I asked, once. It's so that people still have time to go to the pub afterwards, I was informed, without any hint of irony.) We bundle up all the children and most of the adults and are not long into the service before we realise somebody has changed the words. Our long-established childhood comfort of knowing that as soon as we sit on the hard, wooden pew, hymnbook in hand, we will know where we are and what we must do, vanishes in the first congregational response as my sister and I look at each other in horror and mouth the unholy words, "What the fuck?" as all around us people are reciting a new response we do not know. The pope, it transpires, has changed the mass, and we are untethered once more. If even this can change, then what hope have I for finding stability?

"Can't wait to get back and open a bottle of wine," I whisper to my sister.

"One each," she mouths back at me. There is sense in the rural Irish way after all. We stand and sit and kneel when the congregation does, but instead of whispering prayers, we whisper about how soon we will be away from here. The children try not to giggle, and loudly sing some of the words to some of the hymns—not necessarily in the exact place where they are supposed to be sung, but their intentions are good. As we leave, the priest hands out chocolate with his Christmas wishes, and we pile into the cars and head for the house where there will be warm beds for the children, wine for the adults, and stockings for Santa to fill. Christmas is here; there is a flurry of settling snow, and my world is sparkling again.

By somewhere around 2 a.m., the stockings are filled,

wine bottles are emptied, one of my brothers has offered to make breakfast for everyone, and I am drunk.

I am drunk, and therefore I turn away from everyone and text Charles.

Happy Christmas to you all.

I don't write, *Please text me back to tell me you miss me*. I don't tell him there is a flurry of snow that reminds me of the Christmases we had before. I don't say this is not the Christmas I had planned to have. As I send the text, I knock an empty wine bottle to the floor. It smashes into a million broken sparkles, and James tells me it is probably time I went to bed.

CHAPTER THIRTY-TWO

EVERYTHING CHANGES

*T*he holiday gives me time to talk. It is a nice change from only talking to myself about all that has happened. Annoyed as we are by the boys' lack of kitchen aid, my sister and I do not protest as strongly as we should, because it is this space that gives us time to talk to each other. We are interrupted frequently by half-hearted offers of help—which mean far less than the words imply, as they are usually uttered by someone entering the kitchen only to reach in the large and well-stocked fridge for a new bottle of something, or by a hungry child foraging for leftover snacks. My sister and I become adept at halting mid-sentence, switching to mum/sister/wife/aunt, and then seamlessly continuing from where we had stopped once the interloper has retreated with whatever it was they had come for. In this manner of fits and starts, I tell her the story. I admit to her the things I don't say aloud to even myself—the parts where I am in the wrong, the parts where I lost my temper, or my friend, or my husband—and, as I tell her, I feel I may come out of it somehow after all, because, by the end, I was a person I wished to be.

On the Tuesday back in September when the business fell apart, we were on our way to make cider. We were to help a friend, in return for her tuition and guidance. We would go to her place to learn, then bring her equipment home with us, so we could add cider-making and apple-pressing to our 'Orchard in Autumn' repertoire. We had already published a well-received article in the spring where every photo had a candy floss cloud of apple-blossom in shot, with anything from springtime picnics under the trees to swathes of blossom to decorate wedding venues. In spring, the orchard was beautiful, and I was repeatedly drawn to it to take endless photos. My favourite picture showed Charles watering the trees on a particularly hot late-spring evening, but the photo didn't show the moment he'd turned the hose on me. It didn't show the moment I'd pulled off my t-shirt and thrown it at him. And it didn't show the moment he'd wrestled me to the ground, and we'd lain there together under the last of the blossoms until the sky turned to pink and we began to get cold. In the first book, we'd done a whole chapter on 'What to bake on the farm', with apple pies and apple cakes and apple chutneys, but this year, we were adding a new twist. Charles had voiced plans to introduce his own line of cider, and if I had paid attention, I may have realised he was already making contingency plans to distance himself from what we were doing together. *His* line of cider. Not ours. So, on that final Tuesday, our friend's apples were picked, or gathered from the orchard floor, and ready to be pressed, juiced, squashed, and drained until the apples would be unrecognisable, but the remains would be something even better. We wanted to borrow her apple press, and we needed to learn how to use it.

But on this day, it would be Charles and I who would become squashed, drained, bruised, and broken. Rather than apples, it would only be the remnants of our business that would lie scattered in pieces around us. We were in the car, on our way, and had a most almighty fight about something stupid and small. Charles turned around the car, told me the business was over, and pulled over at the end of the lane to the farm and left me sitting in the passenger seat of my own car with the engine still running and the driver's seat still warm from his body.

The night before had been full of anticipation and future; we had discussed the location of a new cabin and made final arrangements for some of the Christmas events. There was hope and promise and excitement, and I was confident we had come around a significant corner. We had spent the evening talking, laughing, and being who we had always been. I was happy, and I was sure we would make it. We were a team, and we would make this work. My feet were up on his chair while he scrutinized the layout for the newest *Weekend Magazine* columns on my laptop. We drank tea together in our easy familiarity while our children were playing together happily, long after their French lesson had ended. Everything was as it should be and as it felt right. The half hour of planning while the children learned French in our office space across the yard soon dragged into three hours of friends spending time together. I was late home again, and James met me at the door with sadness in his eyes. Once again, I could only apologise, but we both knew that while I was sorry for James, I was not sorry for the time spent with Charles.

Hindsight now causes me to wonder if this was exactly what scared Charles most: an evening of comfortable closeness, easy friendship, total understanding, teasing, flirting, sharing dreams, and planning a future—even if that future was dressed up in the clothes of our business and disguised as work. It was a future of continuing together on a business level for a committed time, a series of events, new stories, an ever-increasing audience, and Santa. It was all the excuses and reasons that we needed to spend our days together. It would make a promise to our followers and our readers that Isobel could rip apart in an instant if she were to discover what we had done. I think now that this is what caused Charles to finally do what he did that Tuesday when he pulled out the rug he had placed firmly under my feet only the previous evening.

Or perhaps it was my rage that tipped the final balance and ended it all.

On that September Tuesday morning, when I awoke, I had texted Charles to remind him of a meeting we had planned with the organisers of a promotional event we were committed to attending the following weekend. I texted him to offer to change the time of the meeting to suit his schedule more conveniently. He wanted to buy some hens before cider-making with our friend, rather than take time to attend the meeting first. I can't quite believe it was hens that led to the break-up of our everything. I wonder if he ever did buy any new hens after that; they surely faded into total insignificance thereafter. I can't imagine how new hens would still be important once the end of the business, the end of Isobel's marriage as she knew it, and the end of so much else had happened. But I digress, and it was my offer to fit my day around his hen-buying and my suggestion to reschedule the day's meeting that culminated in his replying that he was not home anyway. He answered my text to tell me that I could not collect him for another hour or so, by which time I would have had no choice but to reschedule the meeting anyhow.

And he could not understand why I was unimpressed that, despite having only confirmed the meeting the night before when we were planning and happy, he could have already forgotten by that morning. I cannot understand either why he did not mention to me the night before that he had to be elsewhere at nine o'clock on a Tuesday morning, despite sitting at his kitchen table on the Monday night agreeing to attend a meeting with me at nine o'clock on the same Tuesday morning. It was another of a thousand occasions when his lack of communication within his marriage became my problem, for the place he had to be instead was at an appointment with one of his children that Isobel had arranged for him but had not told him about. Again. This had happened on many occasions over the past four years—often, he would commit his children to do some work for us, or to be available for a photo-shoot, and then Isobel would take them out for the day instead. I would always be the one to pick up the pieces—rearrange meetings, scrabble around for short-notice alternatives, pull my hair out over it—while Charles, Charles would always shrug and say, "But it was fine," and, of course, it usually was, but only because I had made it so.

So, in the car, that Tuesday morning, on our way to the cider-meeting, having rescheduled the other meeting for the next day and sacrificed his hen shopping to an unspecified "later," I was angry. And I told him so. And he was mad with me for being mad, and there we were, having swung a U-turn across the road and driven home in steaming silence and spluttering rage. In the slam of a door, I was there in the passenger seat with the engine running and Charles was striding down the lane. I leant my head on the cool glass of the window and knew with absolute, hideous certainly that the night before had been another lie. The new articles would not go to print, and the new cabin would not get built, and Santa would not be coming to visit the cabins in the woods.

I followed him. Of course, I followed him. I scooted over the gear stick and into the warm dent he had left imprinted in the driver seat, and I followed him home. He would not get in the car again, so I drove past with intention of beginning to gather the pieces of my four-years-worth of business left in every corner of his life. Once I got there, however, all I could do was collapse onto the floor of our office and cry.

Which is where he found me once he'd walked home.

He calmed down, and I calmed down, and because I didn't know where to start, I didn't start. I sank to the floor and leant against the wall, tears streaking my face. He stood beside me, watching me, sadness etched onto his face. We said little. I think we both knew that this time, there was nothing to say. After a while, he sent me home, but gently this time, because now we were both calmer. I think we were both suddenly so sad and weary from it all. Because he told me to go home so gently this time, in the way of a friend who cares and not as someone who is infinitely frustrated by me, because he was gentle, I went.

"I'm going to call Isobel," he said, through my car window. He looked at me with such grief that every inch of my body longed to pull him into my arms again. "I'm going to tell her, before I change my mind again."

"You can't."

"I have to."

"You can't tell her while she's at work. At least wait until she gets home." He couldn't give her this kind of news while she was working—some things, I still could try to protect her from. Some things. I still wanted to make easier for her.

I think this was the last time he really listened to me.

"You're right. I'll just tell her the business is over, and I'll tell her the rest when she comes home."

"Just wait, Charles. Please, wait till she is home. If you tell her that much, she will know the rest anyway. Please, wait."

But he turned away from me and went into his home. As the door swung closed behind him, I knew then that the only place I could go was to the house I shared with my own family—my own home. Not this other family's farmhouse where I had felt so at home for the last four years.

I sat at my own kitchen table, alone. Because I knew he'd want to know, I called James and sobbed some more. The frustration I heard in his voice that he was in town and far from home, and his assurance that he would come straight away, spurred me only to gather up Jess and her lead and my boots and hit the road. I told James not to hurry home, as I would be *out*. James has told me that was the exact moment when the cracks in our own marriage were suddenly ripped open all over again. It was as if the fragile stitching we had put in place for the past few days, since he had known about me and Charles, was torn viciously into a thousand pieces of broken thread. He, too, realised at that moment that I would be someone different from here on.

Of course, as always, my thoughts were not with James as Jess and I walked. She strained at the lead, pulling slightly, and sniffing interesting things, but still guided my path as I walked partly-blinded by tears. My thoughts, of course, were still there at the farm with the shreds of my life.

Dear Charles,

I am sorry. So very sorry.

And his reply—succinct, but enough for now: ***I am sorry also.***

Enough for now. It didn't occur to me then that would be all I would ever get.

CHAPTER THIRTY-THREE

NO FURY

*W*hen I was all walked out and had nowhere left to walk to, I walked home. James, of course, wanted to discuss it, but I knew this time there was nothing to say. My dreams, my business, my friendship with Charles, and, still sadly way too far down my list, my marriage, were all shattered. I was exhausted from crying, and, at some point in the afternoon, I fell asleep, clothed, on top of our bed, while James sat beside me. Together, apart, we waited and waited for Isobel to get in touch.

Charles's insistence to wind up the entire business in just over a week, including removing everything I wanted to remove and finalising the paperwork, was a heavy weight over me for the rest of that week, especially as I had to continue to pull together to fulfil the commitment we had made to work at the coming weekend. He could not understand why this work was now my priority, or that I needed to still promote the book, knowing I would need the sales. I felt he made it even more my priority by his own choice to walk out on it. If I have no job, no business, and potentially no husband, then I needed to shore up against my ruins and do my best to preserve the dregs of my reputation. I have built my business and my audience on my reputation and my reliability and my standards, and to let them slip at that point would be another shot in my feet for my future. I had committed to our space at that country fair, and I could not—would not—disappoint someone without notice when future work may rely on it. I could not let down a stranger without notice, but Charles could let down his friend and his wife and his family. He let me down and cared little, but I—I was hindered again by my conscience and the integrity Isobel accuses me of having lost, and I would fulfil this job if it killed me.

So that was how I found myself alone in a field on a sunny Friday afternoon at the end of September, with the components and the determination to erect a marquee. An old injury and a lack of the necessary extra two inches of height meant it was near impossible for this one heart-broken girl to do what was normally a job for at least two of us, but fury, despair, and a desperate need to prove myself spurred me on. Despite wasting the first hour of the day by looking for someone who would tell me where to put up my tents, I was eventually surrounded by poles spread across the damp grass, watching my borrowed van threaten to sink into the soft ground. *The van may sink, but I will not.* I turned my back on it in the hope that by ignoring it, it would choose not to sink, and I began to fix the poles together. *This bit I can do.* It was particularly satisfying when I needed to whack the ends with the rubber mallet, because a certain amount of force and fury are useful at times.

The crunch came when I had erected the basic framework, but then needed to lift it to fit in the legs, and to put the cover over. This was not some small tent, but a ten-metre-diameter marquee. The wind was getting up by now, but the tent was not. I was losing the will and the certainty to do this. I sent desperate texts and surrendered to tears.

Dear Charles,

I am overwhelmed by all of this.

I texted a friend to beg for childcare after school, for I now knew I would be there a long time yet.

I am overwhelmed by all of this, won't be home for hours, please, get kids?

I texted James,

Dear James,

I am overwhelmed by all of this.

It was not the first time I had sent James and Charles identical messages. I wondered if this would be another Last Time though.

I texted one of our staff, who had promised to help if she could leave college in time,

Hey, I am overwhelmed by all of this. Will you make it?

Salvation appeared in the form of the site safety officers, who were surveying the area for safety problems and should have been appalled by one girl constructing a large marquee, single-handedly, while her van sank beside her. Instead, bless them, they pitched in and helped. And, in a swift ten minutes, the marquee cover was on; it was upright, the men were banging in stakes for the guy ropes, and the girls were sympathising over my "ass of a business partner" having screwed me over. I was gratified to be able to instantly lay my hands on my first-aid kit when one of the men cut his finger, and the site safety inspectors were similarly impressed with me. This was enough to boost my determination to do this, and do it, I did. By the time my phone decided it would pick up enough signal for me to receive the replies to my texts, and I realised that James was *on my way,* all I needed him to bring was strong black coffee from the garage and some chocolate, for I was standing proud and amazed beside my erected marquee.

Despite my renewed vigour, when James found me in the field, I fell into his arms and clung to him like I was still floundering. Once more, I wished his everlasting ability to save me could only be enough. When the coffee was drunk and I had expressed the gratitude and acknowledgement he deserved for what he'd had to do to be able drive away from work to be my knight in shining armour, I was revived enough for us to battle with the interior of the marquee. We placed tables, chairs, and photo-filled display screens, and a smaller, internal marquee for the stack of books and private head-space space. This tiny marquee should have been easier to erect, as it was smaller, but it was also borrowed, and we had never put it up before. Although its owner tried to tell me how to do it, I was far too distracted by needing to know how to do it to pay attention as to how to *actually* do it. James and I struggled with it together, but, in the end, we got it done. He returned to work, leaving me to finish decorating the space and unload the rest of the equipment I needed. That bit I could do, and by 5.30 p.m. I was confident I was ready enough to call it a day, and I was filled with a huge sense of having proved something to myself.

My phone buzzed with a text from the girl who had promised to help, to say she was on her way, and I was able to say,

It's OK, go home. I did it!
I did it!

CHAPTER THIRTY-FOUR

BREAKING POINT

I cannot make it through a day without something reminding me.

To be honest, I can rarely make it through even an hour.

It seems that every book I read these days has a character with his name in it. They are usually some insignificant bit part, walk-on role, and have little place in anyone's story except to make my own heart leap in my chest and feel sad again for a moment until I realise they are not the Charles in my own story. The Charles in the last book carried a coffin for a few minutes, and then was forgotten easily by the protagonist. To be fair, she had plenty of other problems and traumas, but her problems were mostly called Sean, and although he had an affair with her friend, it all came good for her in the end. She wound up, predictably, with an old love— the love of her life, the one she always felt connected with and felt was truly her soulmate.

My soulmate has gone. He has blanked me, deleted, me, removed me, and lost me.

If someone systematically erases every memory that includes you in it, does that mean it never happened? How can he take my memories along with everything else? He took my dreams, but he cannot change my memory. Can he?

Perhaps, in echoes and predictions from the words of a song, he did not, in fact, take my dreams away—perhaps he has packed them away somewhere, stored with his own. Irrespectively, they seem to have been dumped without ceremony on a high shelf or in a damp cellar, collecting dust and slowly rotting away. I wonder what his own dreams are now. Or if he even dares to dream anymore. Perhaps that is what I gave him for those four brief years—his only chance to dream. Does he, at least, remember that? I cannot imagine Isobel allows him any dreaming now.

I asked his niece how he is yesterday. She said he is "grand." But the rest of her message implied he may not be altogether "grand." She said he is quiet and "strange" with her now—presumably because he knows that she knows, and he knows that she is the only one out of all his family who remains in regular touch with me. She checks up on me and checks in with me with reassuring frequency. I cannot believe how much I still miss them all, and she, at least, allows me to say, "How are they?" now and again. Even if the answer is usually an insubstantial, "Grand."

She said he collected her from the train the other day, and he did not even make small talk, just looked ahead and drove her home, his only flash of life coming as they passed by my house, and he turned to look down my driveway. I wonder if he even realised he had done it, and whether he noticed she had noticed him doing so. I try hard not to turn my head as we pass his fields, ever since my children asked me why I always turn to look. Only a small part of his land borders the road, and to turn to look is inevitably a senseless action. I have never seen him there.

I try to focus my energy away from the farm and my old

life and Charles, and on to my next move at the market. James helps me to build new shelves to fit another, bigger unit I have committed myself to taking. It's good to have his help, and we enjoy having something to discuss that is new and productive. As soon as the market starts up again after Christmas, I will be moving again, front and centre, in direct line with the door. I am ready to stop hiding and ready to be seen. To supplement my increasing range of ceramics, I order in some more toys. The wooden toys that were supposed to be Santa gifts were popular, and sold well, and an old, almost-forgotten dream of owning a traditional toy shop is partly sated by this. I have spent the last bit of the leftover business cash on this new order and am, yet again, taking a chance on trying something new. My clay alone will not support my desire to stay hiding in the market every weekend, pretending to be busy whilst I avoid looking for a 'real' job. Since Christmas is now over, I have had to pack away the nativity figurines and tree decorations, so my stock is very low. I will make more buttons, and more buttons, and more buttons, but there will never be enough to sustain my stall and to fill a kiln quickly enough to fire it on a regular basis, so I am supplementing it with what I hope will catch the shoppers' eyes and keep the customers coming to me while the clay catches up with me again. My stall will be the prettiest in the market and appeal to children and adults alike. I will offer giftware to suit all requirements.

With my new excitement comes worry. The market is quiet now, and its future is uncertain, yet I have paid good money for this stock without any fallback job to pay the bills. I must sell this new stock to cover the cost, and to allow me the luxury of still thumping my clay. I am creating a new range of ceramics to fill the space where Christmas stock once stood, and I have a kitchen full of half-made ideas. I have learned a lot already, and I am confident they will come out good. I am not so confident they will sell.

I have noticed I no longer think of Charles so much when I am making clay, but I focus more intently on creating my pieces. I am beginning to experiment, and push boundaries, and challenge myself. This, I think, must be progress. I wonder, then, if I am getting over things, but then I am not sure if I want to get over him, and I start to remember again, to stop myself from forgetting.

What if I forget him too, and then he does realise he needs me or wants me? I made a promise to him that I would be here for him, always, so although I think of him less when I make clay, I still let him flood into other parts of my day. Jess and I spent the morning walking, and from the minute I pulled on my boots, he was there again, haunting my mind and our freedom, and every passer-by on the road was never him, however hard I wished for it to be.

I am not the only one clearing away Christmas stock. I heard from a friend that Isobel spent Christmas Eve breaking the Christmas ornaments I gave her as a present for another Christmas when we were still friends and loved each other. She gave me an ornament too, and while it didn't hang on my tree this year, it is safe in its box, in case, one day, I want to look at it again. It probably helps that I didn't have Christmas at home this year; perhaps if I had, and we had put up a tree in our home, then James would have found the box as we decorated the tree in a pretence of happy family tradition. He would have gently, carefully, unwrapped the little silver decoration and held it up to sparkle in the fairy lights, before throwing it to the ground and crushing it under his foot until it became nothing but a crumple of broken memories.

I understand why he would have had to do that, just as I understand how Isobel needs to break the things I gave her. I understand this, but I don't understand how Charles can stand by and watch her. Does he feel any kind of remorse, or guilt, or pain, or hurt, or any memory of how carefully I chose these gifts for her, with his help? Does he remember the day I stood beside him in the antique shop in town and helped him choose a most precious gift for her? Does he remember that, once, we made our choices based on each other's opinions? Does he care at all that all the things we did together are broken?

I kick at the stones as I walk the bog path, and I realise with the same sudden fury as it takes to crumple a Christmas ornament or throw a broken piece of clay in the bucket beneath my worktable, that Charles is no longer the person to whom I gave so much, but the person who took so much from me.

Does Isobel really believe that systematically removing or destroying all trace of me will make her forget? I wish I thought it would work for me. There are memories in everything and everyplace—a Paul Simon song on the radio and I'm there in his kitchen, helping his children with homework; a car that looks like his mother's and I wonder if he is driving it; a flash of new green spring shoots forcing their way through the barren ground and I am there in his green eyes, longing for hope. How can he forget it all when I can only remember?

Dear Charles,

You told me it was because you thought you could have everything. (To me, of course, it became my everything.) James said you were foolish, because you hadn't realised you already had everything, and you threw it all away. James said you had a lovely wife, a beautiful family, your own land, a growing business that was fun as well as work. And, and ... you had me. You had me as your friend, your business partner, your playmate, your company, your inspirations, your dreams. You had in me a friend who would do anything for you, and who adored your wife and children too. You had in me a friend who loved everything you gave her—the freedom of your land, the magic of the forest, the big, open spaces, and the chance to build on my dreams. And in exchange for that, I very quickly came to love you all. I felt at home in your home, and I felt like I had become part of your family.

You. You were given this new friend—a present from your wife, if you like—a new toy to play with. She trusted you to play nice and not break anything. And, of course, she trusted me too.

When we agreed to go into business together, we didn't even know each other; we'd had a few exchanges of pleasantries in the school playground, nothing more. I knew who you were—you were the father of children in my children's school, you were married to someone I was sort of friendly with but didn't know too well, you were one of that big family up there at the other end of the village, your children were sometimes in class with mine depending on how the years fell, although none of them were actually in the same school year—I knew who you were, but I had no idea of who you would become.

And then Isobel, poor Isobel, in friendship and help, offered me a project, a space to work from and an opportunity, and then, very quickly after that, an introduction to you and to an exciting new business idea.

It was all down to her that the idea became a reality, over your kitchen table one cold winter day, over the first of a million cups of tea drank in your farmhouse kitchen, when she innocently suggested we could work together on something big and exciting. You, she had told me, had a dream and a space and a plan. I, in return, had a dream and a following and the know-how to paint a struggling farm with a whole new life. Over that first meeting, somehow, just somehow, we found ourselves agreeing to become partners and turn your farm into our business dreams. When I sat down at your kitchen table, we were strangers who knew little about each other. When I left, we already knew that however much we didn't know about each other, we knew enough. We trusted each other, and we trusted Isobel's insistence that we were perfect for each other.

CHAPTER THIRTY-FIVE

SHOP GIRL

*B*efore I even have time to fall headlong into *Confessions of a Market Trader*, the market is closed down by a short-sighted mix of town big-wigs and the council planning department, and I am sinking again. A chapter of my life is yet again abruptly ended before I'm ready to end it, and the pages of my story are turned quicker than I can write them. However, my phoenix can still rise, as I find myself swept along in a wave of "we'll-do-something". A group of optimists are emerging amongst the traders, and they determine to pull together from the ashes of the market and reinvent themselves again as better, classier, and a more up-market market altogether. I am suddenly one of the 'we' and 'we' are re-vamping a shop unit in the heart of the town. We are going to come together—a select few, just ten or so of us out of eighty-odd traders—to build a co-op, a trading hub, an emporium, a treasure chest. We are the Creative Ones: the artisans, the bakers, and the makers. We are the ones with the goods to target the next level of consumers, and we will sell to the people who still have money to spend, despite these dark days of Ireland's recession.

In the weeks between the end of the market and the beginning of the new shop, I had anticipated a time to stop and catch my breath, a time to remember my children and to be their full-time mum again, a time to take Jess on long walks, and to make a million buttons. I had planned to have time to make enough buttons to re-stock the wool shop in town and to meet the demands of a new customer who wishes to use them on her own creations and to sell in her own new shop. I planned to have time to build up a range of repeatable designs and display them beautifully in my new internet shop. And, above all, I planned to have time to catch up with all the friends I have neglected for so long. I thought there would be time for a social life and tea and chat and after-school play for my children.

However, the traders who are pulling together to build our new shop are enthused and motivated. Plans for the new space are racing along, and I am, once more, on a conveyor belt that is taking me for a ride. I feel as if I am on the way to an uncertain destination, but with no chance to step off or even to pause to think things through. I tell myself it is still my best option, and I must do this, for once more, it is better to be *In* than to be *Out*, and I believe this could work for me. Overall, I no longer have anything to lose. Additionally, the rent is low, the location is good, the people are nice, and what else have I got to do with myself anyway? So, I stay on the conveyor belt, to see where it will take me, and there is suddenly a working plan of painting and plastering and sanding down and putting up shelving and cupboards and units. As if that was not pressure enough, I hear myself committing to making shop signs and advertising posters and designing the logo and utilising my press contacts. I can hear my voice saying, "I can do that," even though my head said I mustn't, and before I know it, I am once again drastically over-committed. This develops into stress and yet another chest infection crushing me like a vice and stopping me from glazing my new range of buttons, and now I am behind, and rushing, and the world is closing in once more.

Before I can stop to catch my struggling breaths, we are transforming the new shop space with paint and partitions and handcrafted units and antique wooden tabletops cut into countertops. Within two weeks of the market closure, our new space in town is reborn with elegance and style and undertones of Art Nouveau and twenties' glamour, and we are *Open*.

I wake each day with an uncomfortable mix of excitement and trepidation. Will it work? Will people call in? If people do call in, will they buy my wares? Will I become claustrophobic and confined in my unfamiliar world of shop hours and waiting? And will I miss the great outdoors that has been my playground for the past few years? I am more tired from this niggling uncertainty than I ever was when I was running daily through fields and combining thinking up new ideas for 'how to use a farm when farming is failing' with boundless physical recreation and energetic activity. Each night when I get home, I am thrust into a whole new life that includes the alien activity of ironing, for now, for the first time ever, I must dress like a grown up.

Every. Single. Day.

My jeans and work boots are relegated to a chair in the corner of the bedroom. They have become things I wear on Sundays to walk poor, neglected Jess, who must be wondering where our long walks twice daily have gone. My camera has a thin layer of dust and lays untouched and resented on the drawers in the bedroom. I still can't look through its lens without seeing the things I will never see again. Spring is coming, and the evenings are beginning to draw out, so there are walks for Jess when I have the energy, but not so regular or so far as before, on those long, long in-between days during the transition from Farm Girl to Shop Girl.

If I was wondering whether this could be another corner turned and another step towards the light at the end of the darkness, I was wrong. Already, after less than a full week of trading, I am meeting people who I haven't seen yet since autumn. There are so many people I have not seen since the abrupt cessation of my newpaper columns; or since the desperate submissions of the last dregs of articles already half-formed before the end came, where I tried to honour deadlines and commitments. There are people I have not seen since the flurry of final interviews where I tried to hold myself together long enough to explain to my audience that it was over, without being able to explain anything at all. There are people who know me, who I have never met, or never known, and for them, it's not enough that I have written it, or said it through choked-back tears on the radio, or to have put out desperate, heart-broken, tear-stained posts on social media and national newspapers. It's not enough to have thought I could hide here in the shop and pretend to be someone new. People come in, and they know me, or they read something I wrote, or they heard me talk, or they have my book, or they came to the farm for one of our events, or they recognise my photo from the *Weekend Magazine,* or they think maybe I look like "that girl from the farm." There are more than I ever imagined possible when we began the collaboration of journaling the farm and its growth into diversity. Only a few months ago, I would have been delighted to know how far we were reaching, but now … now they are smothering, grabbing, adding layers and layers and layers to my pain, and chipping away at my attempts to reinvent myself. So instead of being Shop Girl with a repertoire of "How may I help you?" and "Let me wrap that for you," I become the girl who is explaining repeatedly: *Yes, it is me; yes, it's such a shame, no, no, I don't do that anymore . . .* and then, always—always, I become, once again, stuck in conversation where I put my heartbreak on my sleeve and in my voice and in my eyes as I explain. I repeat the same phrases, over and over:

"No, I didn't choose to end it."

"No, I didn't *want* to end it."

"No, I don't live at the farm."

"Yes, Charles is still there."

"No, we weren't married, not to each other. He lives there with his wife." It still surprises me how many people don't know that. Perhaps they, too, were fooled into forgetting that life contained more than just me and Charles.

"Yes, he will stay there—it's his farm, after all, it was never mine—but everything we did together is no more, and no, I don't know what he is doing now." I try not to add that I don't know what he is doing because he will no longer talk to me. And, although I rarely say it aloud, a voice in my head adds, Y*es, oh yes, I miss him every single day, and yes, I still think of him first thing in the morning and last thing at night, and a thousand, a million, a million million times in between.*

I don't know if he even reads the messages I still send to him now and again, when I want to share, or tell, or ask, or laugh, or cry, or shout.

Or when I am scared.

The last message I sent him was on the day I was at the hospital a week or so ago, waiting for a chest x-ray. It seems the crushing weight of my heart and the pressure of a thousand shards of broken-ness are more real than even I realised. The constant struggle to breathe and the chest infections that have recurred too often over the past year ("Chest infections?" Anna had said, with a disbelieving laugh. "Those are stress infections, dear.") and the suffocation of reaching for my inhaler in the dead of another long and sleepless night may, in fact, be the real pain of a broken heart, or broken lungs, or both. I have been referred for x-ray and echo-things and heart monitoring and an acknowledgment from the doctor that stress will not be helping, and she "will sort it out." My doctor is gentle and reassuring, and also very funny. I tell her I have a broken heart, and she assures me that she knows this could be real, because she saw it once on *Grey's Anatomy* on the TV. She laughs then, and tells me that Broken Heart Syndrome, is not, in fact, caused by grief and loss, but is something different altogether. Nonetheless, she acknowledges that grief and loss can cause real, painful, pain, and she offers unconvincing reassurance that I am unlikely to be suffering from anything that time cannot heal. But—there is always a but—as it could be something more serious, she refers me to be checked.

Because Charles has been the person I have shared my life with for so long, I needed to tell him this. I needed him to know how scared I was. I needed to give him the chance to care.

I was ill before. It was a long time ago, when we were just starting out. That time, I told Isobel. She was still my friend, then, and he was someone I was only just beginning to know. Even then, Isobel knew how close we were to become, so she told Charles that I was sick, and urged him to call me to see how I was. That night, he phoned me, and we talked for hours, even though we had barely met and our friendship was still new. So many times since then, we talked for hours, and he gave me sympathy, support, friendship, hope, laughter …

And love.

Way back in times past, back in the days when he was the person who knew me better than anyone, he was always the first person I needed to tell things to, and that has not changed. I do, of course, still have James, and James knows my heart is aching, but it is not a thing we can discuss. I cannot talk to my husband about the pain I feel in my heart, because, although he knows I am in pain, he also knows it is not a pain for him, and I know that he knows, and I am not so cruel as to say it aloud. So now, although James reminds me that he is here for me, I really have no one at all to talk to, because I don't have Charles.

CHAPTER THIRTY-SIX

SHEPHERD GIRL

*B*y eight o'clock this morning, things were going badly. I do not understand why an unfriending on Facebook hits me like a mortal blow, but Charles's oldest daughter has finally dumped me, after six months of hanging in there. And everything hurts all over again. Although I refuse to sulk about something as small as this, it dampens the start of my day. Pulling myself into work mode, I dress in my new role of 'grown up' and get myself organised to go to work.

As I drive into town in my freshly ironed clothes and my grown-up shoes, I try to push thoughts of boots and jeans and messing about in the fields with Charles from my mind and snap into my new life. I try not to turn my head as I pass by the farm, but, of course, the magnetic pull is greater than my will-power, and I gaze longingly across the fresh spring green of the fields with an ache I cannot suppress.

When I arrive in the shop, I am unnerved by the increasing realisation that we have a bulldozer in our midst. One person is calling the shots and making decisions in a workspace built on the premise that we will work together and discuss and meet and have consensus opinions and developments. While she pretends that decisions are mutual, this one person is bulldozing through the rest of us and making changes around us without discussion or consensus. And I will sulk about that for sure.

If I only knew who I am and where I am going and what I want and what I can do or who I can be again, then I would be strong enough to not sulk, and I would stand up and say my piece. Alternatively, I would be calm enough to let it wash over. I would go with a flow and be swept along on a wave of complacency and serenity. But I know none of these things about myself, and I am still wracked with uncertainty and a gnawing doubt as to whether this new Shop Girl life is for me. I do not know yet if I can be Shop Girl, and I certainly do not know if I can work in this environment of a necessary closeness with others. I am sure I cannot work with a definite and enormous gulf between some of our opinions. I keep my head down and busy myself in my own small unit, trying to ignore the movements around me as others redress display units and argue as to whether to leave the door open for welcome, or shut for warmth.

Still, the day is busy enough, and people are beginning to know we are here, and the morning quickly becomes pleasant, as a mix of market regulars and random strangers are lured in by the smell of fresh coffee, fresh-baked patisserie goods, and our attractive window display. The big, loud Italian who runs the café in our little emporium is building us a reputation for good coffee, traditional Italian cooking, and his flirtatious demeanour.

My friend Liz calls in, and I have a lingering coffee break at a window table with her. Despite problems of her own, she has time and sympathy for mine. Perhaps my troubles offer her respite from thoughts of her own failing marriage and necessity to move to a new house. We offer mutual sympathies and condolence and insincere platitudes that neither of us believe, and so the morning passes, and I think the day will get better. However, although it's no longer the time of year when the phone rings with enquiries from those groups who are looking to book to visit Santa, or to book a Christmas break in the cabins in the forest, it is now the time of year when editors are thinking of the next season and want to discuss my predictions and plans and ideas for summer, for autumn, and for times and events stretching into a future I can only guess at. As fast as the day started to improve, it crashes around me once more as I field the umpteenth call, and explain on repeat, "No, Charles has pulled out; I can't do that."

I should be able, as Charles suggested in September when he shattered my world, to leave it there, but instead, I engage in conversations, for these callers are not usually strangers, but the people I got to know over the four years. These are the people who built the business for us and who became, if not friends, then at least friendly acquaintances, and I will be polite, and friendly, and chat for a minute. Even without friendliness, I would make time and talk, for one day, I may need them again. They paid our bills and gave me the outlets for everything we did. I still need the revenue from book sales, and I still need my reputation as a trustworthy voice for those struggling to regenerate their businesses against the recession. I still need my foot in the door for future articles and columns. These small things—these moments of conversations about Charles, and about the things we did together—mount through the day and prevent me from moving on. This endless relay of phone calls merges into a buzz of white noise as they jostle for my attention with conversation with the shoppers and lookers (who come in daily-increasing numbers as word gets out about the shop). This talk, together with the banal chat with my fellow traders, means I now speak to countless people throughout the day, so why, why then, do I feel so lonely?

Dear Charles,

Today I told approximately another forty-seven thousand people that we are finished. Some of them tell me they tried to call you, but you don't answer your phone to them. Please, could you talk to some of them sometimes?

Dear Charles,

I should be pleased to hear it's not just my calls you ignore, and I know it's hard to talk to them, but I can't do this alone.

Dear Charles,

The fields are full of lambs, spring is springing all around me, and I cannot help but think of you.

Of course, he does not answer me, and I do not know if he even reads the messages or deletes them as fast as my name shows up in his inbox. I like to think he reads them still, and I convince myself he is not angered by my comments and news I still share with him. I convince myself he is reassured that I have not cut him dead in the way he has cut me, and I convince myself his lack of answer is silent acceptance that he remembers I was in his life. I suspect that, in reality, he either does not read them, but deletes and hides the evidence of my contact, or he shares them with Isobel, and rages.

Disconcerted by these constant reminders of Charles that serve only to fuel the longing that is always with me, like a weight around my heart, and the worry that changes are being made around me in the shop that I am unhappy about, I leave early and head home. As I drive, I notice that, for the first time since I became Market Trader and then Shop Girl, I am driving home in daylight, and the days are beginning to brighten, and I remember that beautiful spring two years ago which I cannot forget and will not forget and do not want to forget. I only wish he would remember it too.

Although we started to see the glimpses of our growing attraction for each other in those cold, dark, angry October nights when James helped me and Charles did not, or perhaps in the many months before that, or maybe even only six months after the business began, it was the springtime after that October when we finally let our feelings run away with us. At the start of the most glorious spring I have ever known, just as winter was moving out of the way, we started something I thought we couldn't finish … until he did finish it, just when I thought it was real.

That February was cold and frosty, with bright sunny days, blue skies, and frozen nights. On the farm, lambing was in full swing. The sheep were in the sheds, and the waiting game had begun. I'd spent a few days hanging around in the sheds already, camera ready, with my anticipation switched to fully On. I hadn't seen lambing before, except small glimpses at the tail end of the last season when we were still only hashing out the idea of our new venture. I was excited to have the chance to record some of the ordinary day-to-day farming activities as a contrast to the main focus of our usual articles. Most of our business was focused on ways to evolve—how to move away from traditional farming by using the farm for new ideas, to turn around the crisis brought about by recession and change. As these days passed, I saw a new side of Charles. Whereas usually we worked as equals, exploring new ideas together, with lambing, he was my teacher, and I, his willing student. As I learned more, the balance shifted again, and I felt as if the lambing now belonged to Charles and me alone. Other years, Isobel had helped him, but now, she was too busy with her own work, so he was the one who oversaw it all: the mid-night checks, the four-in-the-morning difficult labours, and the elation of success and the disappointment of failures. I was enthralled. I took shot after shot, video after video, and when I had exhausted every angle and every story, I put down the camera and pulled on the long latex gloves instead. It wasn't enough to see it and record it; to write about it well, I needed to actually *feel* it. I wanted to be there with Charles in the sheep pens, on my knees in the straw. I wanted to be watching and waiting, pulling and coaxing. I wanted to be the one rubbing a limp new-born with a wisp of dry straw until it took a breath and got to its shaky feet. So, with the chill in the air softened significantly by the warmth of closeness, I put down my camera, and I watched and waited and pitch-forked silage. I cleaned out bedding and prepared individual pens for the new mamas, and I watched and waited and sometimes stopped for lunch, tea, and chat in the warmth of the farmhouse kitchen. Side by side, day after day, Charles and I warmed our bodies against the range, and our hands around the mugs of tea, and then, back in the barns, we watched sheep and waited some more. As the days passed, we slowly moved closer to each other—a closeness already begun months ago, but now fuelled by elation of new beginnings and sunny days. The brakes were coming off, day by day and bit by bit, and the anticipation was hanging in the air between us, always, and with increasing obviousness. As I finally delivered my first lamb, down in the dirty straw, covered in blood and mucus, the thrill of being an integral part of bringing new life into the barn lit a fire in my very soul. We stood together, watching it take the first wobbly steps towards its mother. Over the last few days, our own steps had also become less wobbly and more confident as we touched more often and lingered on each other's gazes for too, too long. That day, as my new lamb suckled its mother for the first time, our eyes met in that straw-strewn barn, filled with the stink of sheep shit and fresh blood, and Charles saw the tears in my eyes and pulled me into his arms.

A less romantic setting would be hard to imagine, but the tension was becoming undeniable. As those lambing days went on, the increasing quantity of hugs, strokes, or touches after a difficult birth, a twin birth, an easy birth—any excuse would do—was electricity between us. Whenever we stopped to take a break, we'd traipse into the farmhouse, where he would flip on the kettle while I was still kicking off my boots. He'd make tea, and we would collapse, exhausted but happy, onto the sofa in the sunroom. I'd put up my feet on the coffee table; he would not. He always kept on his boots when we stopped for these short tea-breaks, in case he needed to leave quickly for any farmyard emergency. We would sit side by side, tea steaming in our hands, often in companionable silence, but close enough that our bodies were touching. Then, one of the days, his hand reached around my shoulders and rested on my back. And then, before many more days passed, his hand still reached around to rest on my back as we collapsed together on the sofa for a break, but now his hand was under my layers of dirty, smelly, sheep-stained winter clothing, and against my skin.

"Skin on skin," he murmured, not looking at me, but I gave no rebuke. Rather, I felt only the self-same instinct that brought each new-born lamb to its mother in a barn full of sheep looking for their own new-born lamb—the same unstoppable instinct, which felt so right that it happened without conscious thought or plan. It just *was*. It felt just exactly as if things were happening just exactly the way they should.

Over that magical time of new life and hope and happiness and the heightened emotions of birth and death, I became more confident in my own lambing abilities, and found the desire to be present at all times compulsive and obsessive and undeniable. Almost every day for the whole of the lambing season, I was there, in stinking jeans and filthy boots, just as soon as I dropped the children to school. I would often find an excuse to go at weekends too, sometimes using the justification of bringing my daughter, so she, too, could witness the magic of lambing. The rewards were twofold: the thrill of lambing and the thrill of what was growing between Charles and me. Basic instinct. Unstoppable.

We should have stopped it then, but how can you stop the unstoppable?

CHAPTER THIRTY-SEVEN

BROKEN DREAMS

*I*n the new shop, the bulldozer is bulldozing still, and I am uncertain of my position here. This woman who has the unit opposite me is taking over; she is brash and haughty and has a demeanour that sends customers straight back through the door. She's related to the owner of our new space and asserts 'family rights' every time she speaks. She's unpopular and is causing factions to develop. I didn't come into this looking for another complication; I was looking for a quiet serenity to regroup and gather the pieces of my life back together. I've been pushed from my comfort zone and it is no longer exciting, but has become horribly uncomfortable during these last few days.

My days are long and difficult, and at nights, Charles's family haunts my dreams. Never him . . . well, not yet anyway. Perhaps he will come soon—but I wonder if he's deserted my dreams as well as my reality. Is he sending his family one by one to torment me into believing they are still a part of my life? Or is it my own subconscious, acknowledging he is gone but still desperately clinging to what used to be in my life?

Tonight, the one to invade my dreams is his eldest daughter. We are at a festival, a large hilly field, muddy but green, with a pooled lake in a dip. It is crowded with people who I don't interact with but know are there. I'm busy—I'm probably there to work, but in this dream, I'm just walking and watching and being there. Alone. Alone in a huge crowd of festivalgoers and drunks. I've been there before. Back in August, we'd attended an arts and music festival, as part of a media campaign. I spent the second evening wandering around, my erratic paths lit by sweeping, pulsing waves of strobing lights. I walked aimlessly, long into the night, enjoying the music, while Charles and two of his daughters slept in the marquee with a few other media connections we knew. I listened to one of my favourite teenage memories on the main stage, before finally succumbing to tiredness. I stumbled clumsily into the tent, where I crawled, fully dressed, into my sleeping bag a few feet from where Charles slept. It was the morning after when I awoke with the force of his gaze on my face. It's crazy to think that only weeks later, September came around, and our business ended. Nonetheless, that night in the tent was real, but tonight, as I walk through my dream with his daughter beside me, it is just another delusion.

Suddenly in this dream-field of thousands of dream-people, I am no longer alone, but Charles's daughter is at my side. She is cruel and bitter and wants to talk and tell me how much she hates me. I can tell she is aware she should not be talking to me at all. She is uncomfortable in my company, but only in that she does not want to be seen fraternizing with me —the enemy.

But then it becomes apparent to me that she is drunk. Very drunk. Just seventeen, and unaccustomed to excessive drinking, she is staggering and slurring, so now I become her mentor and her protector. In the dream, she has realised this too, and despite her knowing she should not be with me, I can tell she wants to spend this time with me just as I want to spend this time with her. She, too, has missed what used to be. And because it is only a dream, I cannot remember what we do or where we go or what is said or not said, but eventually, I accompany her to where her mother is, and I wait, out of line of Isobel's sight, but close enough to ensure the girl gets safely to where she should be.

Upon waking, I can only grasp uselessly at the comfort of knowing that, in my dreams at least, I will always watch out for his children if they need me. In my dream, I have tried to send them the real message that they will always be safe in my company and can turn to me in need. And although I know it was just a dream, I am reassured that his eldest child, at least, still believes in me enough to spend time with me, even when she knows she is forbidden to.

The next night, it is Isobel herself who visits my sleep. We are walking on the same pavement, and as I walk, she joins from a side road at the exact moment I cross her path, and, as in the previous night when I met her daughter, she is at first angry, uncomfortable, and looking for avoidance. I, too, do not know how to act, what to say, or which way to walk from here. But then we acknowledge to each other the awkwardness of this situation, and after a few uneasy yards in which I cannot recall who is walking in front, behind, or even beside, we chat and part with more ease than expected. She has realised my life has changed beyond recognition, and she knows I know what has become of hers. We are allies in our distance, and as we walk together in my dream, she has come to terms with this. She acknowledges we are both victims of the same fight. Our wounds come from having loved and trusted with heart and soul, and one man has injured us both with the same sweep of his sword. In this dream, I know she has realised this, and although we do not part as friends, we do part having understood each other a little better and with less animosity than when we first met on the street. I do not claim to be able to interpret dreams or to understand them, but can it be as straightforward as acknowledging Isobel and I now travel the same path, as dictated by the actions of the man we both loved?

The dream shifts and changes, and his youngest is there now, running, as she always did, to be hugged and held and loved. I do not know whether to allow the contact and the love we still have for one another to be shown, or whether I must hide it from her mother, who is watching, and push away the child. My question meets Isobel's eyes, and on this matter, at least, she understands me, and I know the hug is permitted but must be brief and with no tears allowed to fall. I have not forgotten I am not allowed to display emotion, and so I play by the rules and give the hug, but then gently redirect the child to her mother, and Isobel and I part once more, again with a greater level of understanding and a faint but definite recollection of the friendship we used to share.

I am bewildered by the meaning of these dreams, one after another, where I am visited by Charles's family. In part, they reassure me, for they seem so real at the time. In part, they sadden me, for I always wake to the realisation I was just dreaming. I wonder why they came, one after the other, night after night. It is strange the middle child does not come, as it is her who haunts my daytime. My own child and this one of his will meet frequently over the next few weeks, as they prepare for the finale of this year's drama lessons. They are in separate classes, but in the same stage school, and once a year, in spring, there are shows and parades and festivals. The time is inevitably drawing closer when they will meet, and we will meet. It is already weighing on my mind in daylight hours how we will act, what we will say, and how angry or cruel she may be to either my daughter or to me. Although I am nervous of her displaying any cruelty towards my own daughter, I am equally wary of her ignoring my child who she was once as close to as another sister.

I could attribute, then, this steady parade of his family into my dreams as a part of the worry I feel about this inevitable and fast-approaching meeting. Or I can blame the full moon, or the time of the month, or the ache in my heart that throbs even while I sleep. But, really, whatever else I try to blame, I can really only blame two people for this haunting, and one of them is me.

CHAPTER THIRTY-EIGHT

TALKING ITALIAN

*I*n the shop, things are not becoming any easier. I must learn the Italian for "I am happy to be your friend, but if you keep leering down my top and touching my breasts, I will knee you in the balls harder than you can imagine," and maybe then Lorenzo will understand what I am trying to explain to him. Lorenzo is the Italian man who runs the little café unit in our shop. He makes great coffee and is without doubt the heart and soul of our new shop. I enjoy his company and am happy to take the friendship and comfort of his arm slung around my shoulders. I'm not, however, happy or comfortable to take his leering. I'm worried by his request, made in halting English, for me to not rush off so fast at the end of the day. Yesterday, he asked me to wait after work. Consequently, I left much quicker than I normally do. I must not allow myself to be left alone with him once the others have all left, and I will be careful to make a quick exit every day from now on, just in case.

I must learn the Italian for "I have a husband, and you have a gorgeous and lovely girlfriend who I like very much, so *I am not interested* in you," and maybe that will help him understand. He doesn't need to know I have, once before, had a friend, who had a wife I liked very much, but whom I was still so very, very interested in, and now I don't have those friends in my life anymore. Lorenzo tells me he can see I'm sad sometimes and that he thinks I'm dangerous. He says he knows I have secrets. I shrug and tell him I'm happy to be his friend, but that's all. He doesn't seem to understand that this time, this time, with this man, I really do mean, "friend," and I really do not mean, "Yes, you can become my dearest and my closest friend who I share so much with that I fall in love, and then we ruin everything, because I trust you and believe your promises, and they are nothing but lies."

And I must learn the Italian for "Please stop with the intense closeness and groping. Aside from making me feel very uncomfortable, it doesn't make us look good to the others in the shop, and I don't want to make more enemies in this new workplace where I already feel out of place." Then maybe he will understand I want to fit in, quietly, and without drama, but that I don't want to get close to any of them, including him. And maybe he'll understand I will not get that close to anyone at all, ever again. And that, although I don't want to get close, I also do not want to be disliked by my new workmates or considered distant and difficult.

I do not want to need to learn the Italian for "Piss off, you lecherous bastard," but I feel I may need to, just in case I need to say it one day and be clearly understood. I would rather just be friends with this man and enjoy his coffee. I know if I'm honest with myself, I allow him to leer and lech and grope, because it reminds me that I'm still desirable. If I'm honest, I'm flattered that Lorenzo wants to look at me and feel close to me, but I know that while the attention boosts my crumbling sense of worth, it's unacceptable and inappropriate, and I must find the words to tell him so and be sure to make him understand.

I know that even if I learn the words and if he hears what I say, I still won't be able to make him understand that if he tries to look into my eyes, or compliments me, or flirts too much, or wants to share his coffee with me rather than let me take it away to my own small corner to drink alone, then he will remind me of the times I had another friend who shared my coffee and gazed into my eyes. I can't make him understand I still have too many wounds to lick and that I will lick them alone. Even with James, I am prickly about my wounds, and don't want him to offer comfort when I'm lost in self-pity.

I am angry again today and am hiding in the little kitchen in the back of the shop to distance myself from the cow who thinks she can take over the shop. She has upset another customer with her rudeness, and I'm not the only one who is fed up with her. I don't want a confrontation though, so I'm having my lunch back here, away from the drama. I'm shovelling leftovers into my mouth with no elegance or dignity, when Lorenzo enters and corners me in the tiny space. Even though my mouth is full, he swoops down upon me, and from somewhere beneath his beard, he deposits a prickly kiss on my face. He is standing between me and the doorway, and I need to pass him to get out. I try to laugh him off, with a gentle shove. He is still in my way. I throw my half-eaten lunch into the bin and toss my fork in the direction of the sink where it clatters against a glass. I tell him to move, and he moves closer. Now, I shove him, harder, and duck under his outstretched arms. I do not look back, but I can't look forward either. I keep my head down, feeling heat on my cheeks and rage in my eyes, as I return to the sanctuary of my own little space. I pretend to busy myself with paperwork behind my counter, keeping my head down as the tears threaten to spill out and smudge my pages. I am grateful for the lunchtime lull, and I can keep my back turned until the shaking stops. I do not speak to Lorenzo again today, although as he passes by on his way from the kitchen to his own space, he steps into my unit to say he is sorry. I do not turn, for I am afraid that if he sees me cry, he will put his arms around me, and I will sob against his chest and allow him to comfort me.

As soon as seems reasonable, I close my unit and leave. Outside, the day is beautiful; the sky is bright and blue, and the sun is warm. The last few days have been nice, and the forecast is good. It is exactly two years since the last Spring of Promise, and I do not want to be reminded of that every day by sunshine and balmy skies. I do not want the niceness of the days to engulf me. I want to be miserable forever because this is who I have become now.

There is a hint of a promise of another good spring not too far from these last days of winter, but it is a promise I will not believe in.

CHAPTER THIRTY-NINE

NOT MEETING

*T*he weeks pass quickly as I move through the motions of a new normality. I go to the shop, come home, work at clay, fire the kiln, and try to find energy leftover for my children in the dregs of my time. I am being pulled in more ways than I can stretch, but I am filling my days. I have missed Charles's company for six months now. I have missed him every day and every morning and every evening and a thousand times in between, but my days are busy, and my mind has to fit in more than just thoughts of him and memories of what I miss the most.

However, with the arrival of our daughters' drama performance week, a meeting was inevitable. The first event we both attended, one April evening in the grounds of a local Georgian manor house, he arrived late, and under cover of darkness. The warmth of the day had drained away, bringing goose-bumps creeping along my skin. Charles stood to the side of the crowd for long enough for me to meet his eyes, but from too great a distance to communicate everything I wanted to say to fill the months of silence. From such distance, I could read nothing in his expression, and I turned away, unable to risk holding his gaze until I lost my breath and my focus and my sanity. Inevitably drawn back to him moments later, I looked up again. Caught still watching me, he nodded the slightest of acknowledgements, and moved to stand somewhere behind where I was sat alone on my blanket in that cold, lonely garden surrounded by warmth and chatter. While I forced my focus forward towards the stage, and our daughters' performances, all my senses reached into the space behind me. With the only lights shining onto the stage, and the rest of the garden thrown into darkness, I could not be sure where he was now. I am sure I could feel his eyes on my back, but, of course, I cannot know he was really watching me at all. By now, I was shivering with the cold, and I was not shaking from the nearness of Charles. I was not shivering from the churning turmoil of knowing he was so close, yet still out of reach. I was not.

By the end of the evening, when I gathered my daughter to leave, sure that now, now, at least, I would see him for real, the darkness engulfed us all, and he was lost to me again. From that darkness, he suddenly emerged beside me on the path, within arm's reach. A touch, a stretch of my hand away, and then he was gone, gone ahead, with a walk too brisk for me to follow without drawing attention to myself. Besides, my daughter had now gone in the other direction, into the crowd, into the night, to find a friend, and although every part of my being followed him, my body stayed firm, torn from my heart again, determined to wait for my child. When she reappeared at my side, and pleasantries had been exchanged with acquaintances and other drama-parents, I took full advantage of the cold to urge my daughter to move quickly. We overtook those walking more slowly and all but ran for the car park, but by then it was too late. He had, once more, slipped from my reach, as if he had never been there at all.

Later in the week, our daughters were again thrown together, this time by a mutual car-share with a neighbour. After the afternoon's performance for a care home, they slurped milkshakes companionably in an after-show cafe, together in a group, and my child seemed grateful for this small reminder of what normality used to be. Despite my shameless interrogations, she admitted nothing except the fun of a Skittles-flavoured milkshake and a car ride with another girl separating our children on the back seat of the lift-giver's car, and this day became another non-event that I desperately tried to make into something more.

And then, and then . . . in the theatre itself . . . the final show . . . the culmination of a full week of our daughters dancing around each other, their separate classes and differing ages making avoidance easy, with them never on stage at the same time. Yet, by some twist of the plans I'd made in my fantasies where Charles was allocated seating behind me, next to me, or directly in front, he and Isobel were in fact seated at the other end of the row of seats James and I occupied. If Isobel leant back in her seat, and I a little forward in mine, I could look down the row and watch him, until he too sat back so his wife would block him from my sight. He looked nowhere but forwards in all the time I watched, but the possessive weight of Isobel's hand on his knee was something I could see clearly in my mind even after the lights went down, and the show had begun. I could see her hand there, resting on his leg, because I can feel exactly how my own hand had rested on his thigh every time we travelled together in the car in the space of those short three months that were as long as any lifetime. I could feel the weight of her hand on his leg as clearly as I had felt his hand on mine, time after time, day after day, and I knew its warmth and its pressure and its touch. The darkness of the theatre meant I could remember his hand on my leg as clearly as her hand was on his now, despite there being seven or eight people sitting between us, and despite the undisputable fact that we were, once again, at the opposite ends of the same story.

Throughout the evening, he made no acknowledgement of my presence. James told me that I looked beautiful. I had selected my dress with uncharacteristic care, knowing it was one I looked good in, and did not dispute his compliment. Instead, I did not reply. I couldn't acknowledge to James that I had dressed to impress, but not to impress him. I couldn't admit to him that from the minute I chose what to wear, I was screaming, "Notice me, Charles. Notice me, please notice me," and I certainly didn't admit that maybe, just maybe, he hadn't noticed me at all.

CHAPTER FORTY

BITTER

*C*harles told me once, last summer, that I seemed so bitter now. I laughed. Bitterly. And then I explained that once a girl's best friend has kissed her as if he really meant it, and looked at her as if he really cared, and held her hand as if it fits perfectly and understood her dreams, then told her she has been the glue he needed to fix his marriage, then yes, she will be a little bitter. That'll be me, then; bitter and twisted as a gnarled lemon tree, with lots of nasty little pips in, and deep twisted roots that go down a long way. Since the end of our business, I have only become more bitter. It makes me selfish and judgmental in ways I think I wasn't before, and it has made me wary of trust. I know this, because even on a bright day in the summer where I have escaped from the shop early and all should be well in the world, I am judging strangers.

My daughter has a swimming lesson today, and as James is working a day shift, it's my turn to bring her. In my determination to not be late, I am three quarters of an hour early. I've juggled things around to ensure my son can get home; my unit in the shop is overseen by the kindness of the others, and I have left time to put petrol in the car. The sun is shining, and the sky is as blue as a storybook summer. It feels as hot as the summers I remember from childhood. On this bright, warm day at the end of a mild April, everything seems possible, and I'm so happy to have claimed this extra time for my child.

The swimming pool is in a new complex, with a freshly landscaped garden and play areas. My daughter is happy to have unexpected playtime in the sunshine, and I am happy to have unexpected time to watch her being happy. She flits from the larger equipment to that designed for smaller children, and I am reminded again of the baby she still is, which conflicts with the child she wants to be and the teenage years that are almost within her reach. As she runs for an empty swing, I sit at a picnic table and soak up the sun.

This hot sunshine has brought every possible combination of parent and child to this park, and although nostalgic for the baby I see in her today, I am grateful that, in reality, my daughter is no longer one of the toddlers who persistently run through the gates or in front of the swings. I am glad too that she is not the child sitting on the other swing seat, who plaintively calls to her distant parent, "Mama, pushing me. Mama, *pushing* me. *Mama,* pushing *me!*" My new, more selfish self will not get up to push this other child, but I do still look around for the 'mama' she needs so desperately. My own daughter swings easily, working her long legs up and down and settling into a neat rhythm which swings her higher and higher. I do not even call out to her to show the smaller girl how to work the swing for herself, as I once would have done, but instead, I force myself to relax in the sun and turn my gaze from the struggling girl.

Everywhere I look, people are eating ice-creams. There is much bare skin on show, a sight rarely seen in Ireland, even in the summertime. A beautiful young mother sits a short distance from me, on the other side of the fence, in the area secured for smaller children. She is oozing sex appeal, in the shortest of shorts and a tan to die for, and I assume her to be from somewhere else on the continent, where this heat is normal. She barely looks old enough to have a child of her own, and the children she seems to be with are self-sufficient but not yet old enough to stay the right side of the gate. As I watch them, they run onto the path. Again, I resist my urge to jump up and send them back to the confines of the fenced play area, and I simply watch as the youngest runs across the grass towards the carpark. The beautiful mother deals with her runaway children in a totally unselfconscious manner, which I try not to envy: she stays exactly where she is and shouts across the park, "Kiara, Tanika . . . Kiara, Tan-*ika*, Ki-*ara, Tan-eee-ka!*" and eventually, the children interpret this correctly and return to the safety of the play area. Another mother, this one the mother to a grossly over-weight child, valiantly wins herself points for good parenting in my omnipresent lazing-in-the-sun, people-watching assessment of the humanity around me. This mother urges her whining child to "get on by yourself" and "have a go." I can't guess whether her refusal to help her daughter is due to the mother's own laziness (matched easily today by my own laziness) or a real desire to see her dumpling child burn some calories, but I am willing to agree that trying to "get on by yourself" is what that child needs. The child tries, and fails, then asks her mother again for help. The mother, again, refuses, and the girl tries and tries again until she manages to successfully pull herself onto the climbing frame. I want to cheer for her, as her pride at her achievement lights her face. Her perseverance makes me wonder how we learn when to keep trying and when to give up.

We still have half an hour of playing (my daughter) and people-watching (me), and I don't remember the last time I had the luxury of this nothing-time. I feel I should be interacting with my child, but she is content and smiling and swinging herself still higher. "Mama, *pushing* me?" is still swinging her legs in futility, her mother nowhere in sight. Ms Beautiful Sexy Tan is now off her bench and chatting to Mrs Navy Tights, whose legs, Navy Tights confides, are so pale that even though the temperature has hit the higher twenties, she is too shy to display them in case a stranger in the park judges. Little does she know I am judging her regardless. I hate who I have become.

I do love that I have the time today to be this person though. I love that I am here with my daughter, relaxing and happy—especially today, on what may yet be the only day of real summer we see this year. Mrs Navy Tights has a communion child at the end of May, and seeks advice from Lovely Tan. As I shamelessly eavesdrop, it transpires that Lovely Tan is as Irish as Guinness, and is, in fact, a local beautician. She will spray-tan Mrs Navy Tights for only €15 if she comes in this week. If Mrs Navy likes it, then the usual rate is €25 a time, and she will look radiant for her little darling's communion day. I am amused, as I am every May, by this obsession with fake tans for weddings and communions. (I had, of course, tried to look good for my own daughter's communion last year by wearing drop-dead gorgeous shoes, but I was tanned enough from the days I had spent running around the fields in scruffy cut-offs and skimpy vest tops. The Gorgeous Shoes were about six inches high, and I couldn't walk in them. I discarded them for bare feet just as soon as Charles had seen me wearing them, and about five minutes after, I nearly fell over while walking the two-metre distance from my back door to the table in the garden, but I did not *ever* consider a fake tan.)

The scene shifts again in our sunny park, and 'Mama' appears from almost nowhere to finally push her daughter. I am impressed by the persistence of the child, who has refused to relinquish her hold on the swing for a good ten minutes whilst waiting for the pushing. 'Mama' has another child in tow, and pushes the swing for a few seconds, before tipping the child off and claiming the seat for herself. The child clambers onto her lap, and the second child pushes them both. What I see before me now is a happy family unit, shrieking with laughter and having the best fun of their lives in a sunny park on the first day of summer in a community full of mixed-up lives and people from everywhere and anywhere, all united by sun and children and having nowhere better to be this afternoon.

If I had only now arrived at my picnic bench, this is the snapshot I would have had of this little family, with no hint of the image I constructed five minutes ago, where a neglected child screamed for an uncaring mother. It hits me like a stab in the back that a person can judge someone in five minutes and get it very wrong, or they can know someone intimately for four years and still get it just as wrong. My time here has run out, and as I gather my own beautiful child for her swimming lesson, I wonder how a person can ever really know anything about anyone, however well they think they knew him.

CHAPTER FORTY-ONE

BORROWING CHARLES

I have an old injury; I broke my shoulder many years ago. Sometimes I forget about it for a while, and then something aggravates it, and the pain returns with a vengeance. Sometimes it only bothers me first thing in the morning or last thing at night, or sometimes a small thing, such as gardening, will remind me it hurts.

This is how it is with Charles now. The summer has passed, and we are heading out of another autumn. I've spent more time with my children, and James and I have settled into a new routine. We don't mention what happened, but he supports me with his usual quiet strength as I try to find my way forward. I no longer think about Charles every second of every day, but most days, something will still remind me of the pain. It might be a song I hear on the radio, or the scent of silage in the air. It might be a red car that could be the one he might be driving, or a glimpse of Isobel as she drives by when I am walking with Jess. It might be a fleeting moment, a pang or a longing that stabs me under my ribs when I least expect it, or it might be a mutual friend mentioning his name. Nonetheless, it is not so constant as it used to be. I don't want to forget, but I am beginning to realise I can't remember it all the time either.

But as fast as I tell myself that I am beginning to forget; to move on; to get over it all, it is as if he hears my thoughts once more, and suddenly, my nights are filled again with visits from his family. For a third consecutive night, his family haunts my dreams. This time, finally, it is him. I have been waiting for him, and in this dream, he acknowledges that he, too, has been waiting for me. He has tried to move on and to forget and to erase me from his thoughts and memories, but it has been a pretence and a farce, and, above all, an impossibility. He admits now that he has missed me and all I was to him, and that I, too, haunt his dreams. He takes me by the hand, and leads me to Isobel, where he announces to her that he cannot be without me after all. As always, Isobel has her own piece to say, and she announces that this is impossible, for Charles is hers. He holds my hand firmly, and I cling to his, as if only he can guide me home. I am standing slightly behind him, protected from Isobel's anger by the shield of his body, but, even so, I cannot face her taking him from me again, so I wake up. I lie in bed, willing myself to return to where he was holding me. Once again though, my own will is futile, and I wake properly. Even awake, I can still feel the fit of my hand in his, and the weight of my heart also held firmly in his hands. But all else vanishes, and once more, he is nothing but the fading of my dreams.

The dream lingers with me as I move through the motions of my day. I left the shop a few months ago, unwilling to work amongst the drama there, but I still work at the clay, selling pieces as commissions and gifts to the customers I met in my time in the shop. I have also begun to return slowly, tentatively, to my camera. I'm trying to document this new journey I have been treading—the one where I learn how to create new things from clay—and I'm negotiating with an old contact about ideas for a new book, but the remnants of my dream pull me back to a place I can't move forward from after all. I can't focus on the clay or the future. Unsettled, I pull on my boots, grab the lead, and call Jess. For the first time in a while, as we walk, tears blur my path. I wonder if it is true that if someone visits me in my dream, I am present in his. I want it to be so. If he dreams of me too, it's not over yet, and a sliver of hope shines through the clouds of this dull day.

Jess and I walk for miles, trudging the damp November paths. The despair of the last November, when it was all so fresh and raw, wraps around me like the mist in the air, and self-indulgence brings more tears. We find ourselves at the end of his road, beside the little church on the hill. It seems that my feet—or Jess—know which way I want to walk even if I don't consciously make that decision. When I look up and realise how far we've come, I force myself back to common sense, and instead of going farther towards him, I open the little iron gate and enter the churchyard. I find a bench to sit on, tucked against the stone wall of the church. It is cold and damp, but it suits my mood. I sit there, thinking of everything and nothing, until Jess whines softly at my feet, reminding me to move on. We turn for home, cutting across an empty field to avoid the road. I don't want to chance seeing Isobel driving by today. I come out at my own bog lane, but somewhere along the way, I have lost Jess. She ran off into the mist as we walked aside a babbling stream, and now the fog softens my calls. My voice dissipates into the air as if I said nothing at all, and I think she won't hear me however loudly I call her name. I imagine myself as a sad and lonely figure, a ghost of the person I used to be, and think that even if Isobel did drive by, and did happen to glance across the fields instead of keeping her eyes on what is important, she would see right through me this time. My coat and scarf match the dull shades of autumn, and the mist swirls around me like a dream. Perhaps I am no longer real.

I know I am still breathing because clouds of grey breath mingle with the clouds that blur in my eyes and hang in the misty air. Jess has not reappeared, so I trudge along the bog lane without her, wishing I would learn to keep her by my side, tied firmly to me so she can't leave me. Without her to anchor me to the day, I suddenly have a clarity as to how the story will end for me. This ending will change the chapters of the life of my husband, who has done nothing wrong except to love me unconditionally. This ending, I have realised, will change the chapters of my children's story too, and I feel desperately sorry, for I love them dearly and with a passion that hurts. I know I have failed them, and let them down, and fallen too far into my own despair to take notice of their own, but I know too, as I call one last futile plea to Jess to come to me, that some things simply don't come back.

I realise too now, that the trouble with borrowing something from someone is that you *do* have to give it back. And sometimes, if you don't want to give it back, the person who it belonged to just takes it from you, and makes damn sure you can never borrow it from them again, and you are left with a sense of loss from which you do not know how to recover. You just know you will never be quite the same again. I reach home, without Jess, and go straight to the damp, musty shed I called my studio on more optimistic days than this one.

I have a new bag of clay—better, stronger clay, which I can manipulate and stretch and bend and twist and pull until it nearly breaks. It is stronger and better than I am, for I am already stretched to the point of breaking. I will make better things than I have ever made before, and I will leave them as a legacy to be desired and coveted and loved. I will put the last remnants of my heart and soul into this new clay, and I will make something amazing from it.

After several long days of pulling and kneading and stretching and moulding and coaxing and visualizing and shaping my dreams into something tangible once more, it is done. I have worked late into the nights, and sometimes I have only crawled into bed after the sun has risen and the children are at school. I have barely crossed paths with James for days, exchanging non-conversation, half-formed pleasantries only as we sat together at the table to eat. I have gone through the motions of collecting the children from school, of helping my daughter with homework, of pretending we are a complete and functioning family as we eat and talk about banalities, but as soon as the plates are cleared, I rush to the sanctuary of my workspace and work until long after everyone else is sleep.

Jess did not come home, and I read the loss like a signpost, urging me on to a new place where I can't lose anyone else. My children are bereft again, but I am not the person who can comfort them. I can't even comfort myself anymore. It is James they turn to now. I tiptoe into my daughter's room at night, drop a kiss on her sleeping face, and creep out again so as not to wake her and shatter her dreams. My son, too old for kisses and night-time watching, sleeps soundly behind his closed bedroom door. I stand outside it, leaning my head against the doorframe, willing myself back to the time when they were younger, and when I was nothing but their mother and James's wife. I wish and wish and wish I could go back to then. If James is home, and not on a night shift, I sometimes make it into our still-shared bed, and lie silently beside him, our backs turned to each other and a gulf between us that we can't seem to cross. It is easier to sleep when he's not there, and I don't have to lie there, trying not to reach for him or pretending to be asleep if he reaches for me.

Despite my pain at the neglect I am piling onto my family, I'm proud of what I have created this week. A phoenix has arisen from a lump of clay, fired once and now painted with glaze. It's ready for its second firing—the magic that will fire the glaze into vivid oranges and reds. His plume is delicate, and his feathers are painstakingly carved into intricate patterns. He is beautiful and the most perfect thing I have ever created. I've placed him carefully back into the kiln, propped with supports to stop him falling over while he fires. Now, I set the dials for this final firing.

I have made a mug of tea, only for myself, with only my own fingers to squeeze out the tea bag and no one here to share it with. I sit here in my studio shed, my feet propped on a box, and now I have letters to write. Already the kiln is beginning to heat, and I can smell the fumes as the glazes work their magic behind the firebricks of the kiln wall. I expect, as it gets hotter, I will need to move away, as it will become too hot to bear. If I leave my letters too close, they will incinerate to a substance beyond even ash, and no one will ever read them. I must be careful not to leave them too close to the kiln when I have finished writing them.

Dear Charles ...

Dear Isobel ...

The hardest ones, then: *Dear James* ... and one each to the children. How could I choose this ending for them? How can I do this to them all? The room is already comfortably warm, as it's tucked under the eaves of the old barn, and in the shadows of trees, and I am almost as comfortable as I would be if I was laying in the hammock under the apple trees in an orchard a few miles up the road, in the warm, bright sun of a beautiful spring I remember from almost three years ago. I slump into my chair, lay my head on my arms, and let the memories fill me.

Even if I have to move away from unbearable heat, the fumes and the gases from the glazes will soon begin to penetrate the air of this small room. As the kiln gets hotter, the fumes will strengthen. I hope I will fall asleep first, before the poisons irritate my throat and tempt me to move away, to make a break for outside air. I hope and I hope and I hope I will fall asleep first, and that my dreams will be happy ones. As I drift into sleep, my thoughts are with Charles. I don't want to give him back. Even now, a year since I saw him last —and longer again since we were friends—I'm not ready to give him back to Isobel. I wonder if Charles will recognise me again if I meet him one day far from now in another place. I think he'll always know me. He'll know me from the heart on my sleeve and the chip on my shoulder.

CHAPTER FORTY-TWO

UP FROM HERE

Three years later

It wasn't the first time I didn't know enough. The warning that came with the kiln, and the glazes, and the clay about fumes and heat and poisonous gases were over-dramatic. They didn't poison me or burn me at all. On that dark, cold, November night, I simply slept for a while in the warmth of my studio. I woke, a few hours later, warm and cosy from the heat of the kiln as it fired my phoenix, but with a crick in my neck and an ache in my back. Despite the aches of an uncomfortable sleeping position, I'd woken feeling as if I'd slept well for the first time in months. Years, perhaps. I woke with lingering thoughts of Charles pushed aside by a bright, winter sunrise lighting the floor of my studio in shades of blood and fire, and as I watched the glow spreading across the floor, I felt a flame rise in me. Maybe it was the sleep, or maybe it was waking for a day I thought I had chosen not to stay for, but as the sun rose, I felt as if there may still be something to cling to—something that wasn't Charles.

The kiln would take many hours to cool, so the phoenix had to wait. I could rise without him, perhaps. I eased the kinks from my back and went to the house. The house was quiet and solid in the morning haze. Everyone inside was still silent and sleeping. James was accustomed now to finding my side of the bed unslept in, and to rebuffs if he came to find me while I worked; he would have slept well without me there beside him. The previous year had taken its toll on him, and he was exhausted from it all. The children also would not wake for hours yet, enjoying Saturday hours. James was off shift for the weekend and would have had no alarm to wake him that day. Enjoying the quiet, and the rarity of witnessing this spectacular morning dawn on the final day of what had been a particularly dreary and draining November, I made a pot of tea. The sun shone through smeary windows as I waited for it to brew, then poured it into two large mugs—one for me, and one for James. Treading softly so as not to wake the children, I climbed the stairs to our bedroom and to James.

So much time has passed now, and not enough. The shop closed shortly after I left it, less than a year after opening. I carved a small niche for myself by taking what I had learned from my time in the market and in the shop, and I sold commissions and special orders. I put more time into journaling about the way I learned to take my pain and my anger and turn it into something to sell. I used the contacts I'd had from my old life to regenerate my old column in the newspaper supplement. I never did explain to my readers why the transition had occurred, and some old followers, not liking the change of direction, complained and stopped reading. In their place, I gained new followers, new readers, and, eventually, a new market for the new book. I turned my focus from *Things to do on a farm when farming isn't working*, and, instead, sold a new line of *How I went up from down*.

Putting my time into my photojournalism was less exhausting, both mentally and physically, than the year I had spent trying to be something else I never wanted to be. As the days passed, and I once again had a steady income, some of the worry left me. I still thought of Charles, of course. But now, I thought of him at random, sporadic times, in fleeting and unexpected moments. Sometimes the memories hurt, like a slap to a face in a lead up to Christmas, or sometimes they left a loitering imprint, like a long-awaited kiss in the snow. I had seen Isobel a few times too by now: at the school fair, at a Christmas carol service, at the school fair the following year, other events, other places, as time rolled on. Our two youngest children always fell upon each other and embraced like the sisters they used to be, and Isobel and I passed polite, if not quite friendly, words between us.

We never mentioned Charles.

"How are the children?" "How's your mother?" The weather, the new schools our youngest had transferred to— separately, this time—and the universities our oldest ones have gone to.

I've passed Charles in the car a few times—only a few. Strange, when I think how often I used to see him. Even when we weren't working together, spending every day together, attached and inseparable, I would see him around. I used to pass him if I was driving to town, see him in the school playground, bump into him in the supermarket, but since that last, ugly meeting at the bank a lifetime ago, I don't see him anywhere. I guess Isobel keeps him on a tighter rein, these days. Or perhaps it is his choice; perhaps he is scared to roam, in case he meets an old friend he used to know, or a new friend he may get too close to.

I've settled into a new routine, now I have the time at home. It's come too late for my son, who has left and gone abroad for university. Perhaps it has come too late for my daughter too. She rarely speaks of the loss of Charles and his family, but I know it impacted her greatly and tore her from all she had known for so many formative years of her childhood. I know she realises it is something we don't discuss, but I know it hurts her still. Like my own pain, I presume it has become an occasional ache reminiscent of my old shoulder injury. I don't think about it often, but if I move in a certain way or hear a certain song, the ache calls at me, like a soft echo of the past.

It also came too late for James. We salvaged enough to get through the last three years, and then he left me. He met someone he believed in enough to love with all his heart and look at the way he tried to look at me. I'm genuinely pleased for him. He deserves to be with someone who wants him as much as he wants them. He deserves to be loved fully and intensely. I hope he has the passion and the fire that I found with Charles. For three years after I sat alone in my studio, waiting for my phoenix to poison me, James and I rebuilt our relationship on new foundations. He continued to give me his all and was, as he had always tried to be, my rock and my lighthouse. He cheered me on as I got the new book deal, and as my column in the papers took on a new life. He liked this new column better than the old one, as in this one, I talked about the strength he gave me as he helped me tackle new problems and learn how to create increasingly challenging sculptures to share the workings of. I appreciated him more than I could tell him. Nonetheless, although we had let love grow again, slowly, tentatively, the damage was rooted in us both. During the worst of it—the autumn when I finally admitted to my affair with Charles—James, in his own despair, confided in a colleague at his work. Eventually, as I noticed he mentioned her more and more, he admitted they had become increasingly close, and he wanted to move on. I like that we talk now about more than who will buy milk or toilet roll, and I like that we have things in common again, albeit his new relationship and the excitement he feels in beginning over. I'm happy for him, but as I see how happy he is now, it reminds me of how sad I still am that it didn't work out for me, with Charles. It's when I see James so happy, that I remember most intensely the time I had with Charles. Along with the sadness for what I have lost, for what I threw away, I also feel some relief. Now that I know James is happy, some of the burden of my guilt finally slipped away. We'd become more like friends after the years of being distant and the months of growing closer again, but I could never fully give myself to being his lover. We went through the motions, and I tried to forget Charles, but James and I both knew that however hard we tried, the ghost of Charles would always linger in our bedroom, ever-present in my thoughts and dreams.

I think I will always dream of Charles. It has been about four years now since I saw him last, yet he still visits me sometimes in my dreams. Isobel does too, but with far less frequency. Now, when I dream of them, it takes me by surprise, but I still wake with the weight of loss pinning me down, like a too-heavy duvet. If it's Isobel I dream of, I push off the covers and get out of bed. If it's Charles who comes at night, I lie there, willing myself to fall back to sleep, allowing the duvet to hold me there, wishing, still wishing, it might be true, and if only I can go back to sleep, it will all be real.

James knew this, I think, although it was never said. This is why I am pleased he has found someone who truly loves him, and I wish him well. We have become friends again, although we speak less now the children are older.

I try to use this gift of time to make amends to my daughter. I am wracked with the knowledge that Charles and I stole something important from her and from her childhood. I try to make it up to her, and we spend a lot of our time doing things together. We go to concerts; we travel; we visit family and long-forgotten friends in far- flung places, and during these times, I feel as if she may forgive me after all. She has adjusted well to James moving in with Claire, and she likes to spend time with them both. Our son, too, never mentions any of what has gone before, but I think he is happy and well, and James thinks the same. We see him rarely, but his visits home are shared between us without animosity or discomfort. I cannot help but like Claire, for she has given James what I couldn't, and I love her for that. She gives my children something I forgot to give them while I allowed the distraction of Charles to matter more to me than my family, and for that, Claire has earned a share of them all.

I quite like spending my days alone now. I have things I want to do, and I find ways to fill my time, but my evenings are for my daughter. She doesn't often demand my attention —perhaps she remembers a time she needed it, and I didn't give it—but I ensure I am there. In little more than another year, she will go into sixth form. She is thinking of living with James and Claire, closer to the school, and in the hub of a community. I won't try to stop her. It makes sense, and she is not really mine anymore. I sometimes wonder if I will be lonely, and I think of getting a new dog. I wonder sometimes what happened to Jess way back in those greyest days when she left me, and I wanted to leave us all.

Today something happened that I thought would happen years ago, and then thought would never happen at all. I met Charles in the bank. I didn't realise he was there until it was too late to turn and leave. We made small talk about nothing, and I don't know if he noticed how much my hands were shaking. He said, "Goodbye," and called me by name.

"Goodbye, Charles," I am sure my own voice betrayed the years of anger and hurt and sadness, but it wasn't until I sat shaking in my car outside the bank that I remembered *Charles* was only the name I'd borrowed, to remove him from my reality, for the past four years. I had accidentally forgotten his real name, and I had called him by the one I stole from someone else. I realised, as I drove from the carpark and into the traffic, that, despite the tears that fell onto the steering wheel, I have finally fictionalised him. He is no longer real.

Except, when even now, he still visits my dreams.

CHAPTER FORTY-THREE

STRANGER THINGS

*M*y daughter and I are travelling home. We have spent six weeks of the summer travelling around England, visiting family and old friends. We spent a week with her brother, and a week with my parents, a few days with my sister, and overnights with each of my brothers. We met cousins we haven't seen in years, and visited tourist attractions as if we were real tourists. We ran around London and in and out of the museums and on and off the Underground, as if we were on a timed mission to get our full money's worth from all the capital has to offer during the five days we'd allocated to an expensive London hotel. We have enjoyed each other's company like we haven't for years, and I have seen a genuine happiness in her as we have jumped from train to train, from spare room to sofa bed, from grandmother to third cousins to childhood friends.

I am happy to have shared this time with her, and it feels as if I have found my daughter again at last. While I would not wish to undo the time I spent with Charles, I would give anything to undo the months in which I did not give my children their mother. That, above everything, is my lasting regret. When I lost so much of myself, along with the man I loved and the man I should have loved, my children lost so much too. They had lost the family whose house they felt at home in, the children from that other family who had grown as close to them as siblings, the playground of farm and forest, stream and fields, which they had grown to love as if it was their own, and they had lost Isobel, who was like an aunt to them. Above all, they, too, had lost Charles, who I believe they loved almost as much as I did. While I was busy trying to hold myself together in the aftermath, I wasn't strong enough to hold my children together too. How could I answer their questions when I couldn't even answer my own questions? How could I acknowledge their tears when I couldn't see through my own tears?

And so, although my son has gone, and lives his own life as a new adult, far from home, and seems happy, my daughter has lost too much. On this trip, I think we found some of it again. We talked. (Not about that, of course; never about that.) We laughed. We made plans and decisions together, and as we dozed on long train journeys from one side of Britain to the other, she let her head fall onto my shoulder and trusted I would keep her safe while she slept.

Now, finally, as our summer comes to a close, we are finally travelling home.

It's my turn to doze at we rattle across the North Wales countryside, on the last leg of our journey towards Ireland. This final train of our journey lulls me into an easy sleep, as I know there is no danger of missing our station on this route; the train terminates at the ferry port, and everyone must disembark. My daughter, conversely, is too excited to sleep. She is looking forward to going home, to catching up with friends, and to seeing James after a long summer away.

When we arrive in Holyhead, she tells me about the

people she noticed: the family who talked incessantly about the sea as we raced alongside the Welsh coast, the girl who had a long conversation with a friend on the phone, and about the man who had passed through the carriage with a hot drink in one hand and a Nikon camera that resembled my own swinging from a strap around his neck. I, usually the unabashed people-watcher on every train we'd been on, had missed them all.

An hour or so later, as we are herded through the check-in and into the windowless waiting room, she notices the man with the camera again, and nudges me to look. I am in an intense discussion with a pair of Americans about the primitiveness of the facilities here, and although I turn to follow my daughter's gaze, I can't see who she means. We are called to the bus, and we are moving as fish in a shoal, crammed together with fellow passengers as we bottle-neck in the doorway.

As we spill into the openness, the crowd surges towards the bus directly in front of the doorway. I feel smugly travel savvy as I gently push my daughter towards a second, empty bus, waiting behind the first. Only one other passenger has the same idea, and we follow him onboard, laughing with the driver as we stash our bags. My daughter shoves me in the ribs and hisses in a too-loud whisper, "Him," and I realise the man we followed onto the bus is her Camera Man from the train and the waiting room. He, too, stops to talk to the driver, choosing, like us, to stand close to the front door as we are joined by other passengers who enter from the wider middle doors, and then jostle for the seats in the body of the bus. I have, by now, reverted to my usual travel persona of 'I'll talk to anyone when I'm on public transport,' and shamelessly thrust myself into conversation with the driver and Camera Man. It's an unusually nice day here in Holyhead, and as I chat with the driver about the rare glimpse of blue sky and a calm sea, Camera Man turns to give me his full attention.

"You're local?" he asks in a down-under accent I can't quite place.

"Depends on what you call local," I answer, and explain I'm English, travelling home to Ireland, but not Welsh.

The driver laughs at this, his own Welsh accent a clear give away to his own locality.

"How about you?" I ask Camera Man. "Oz or New Zealand?"

My own camera is stashed in my luggage. I have been using it more and more, but it is not yet the part of me it used to be before I gave all my parts to Charles, but Camera Man seems impressed and surprised that I can talk intelligently about his. My daughter spoils it by interjecting that I have the same one, and that I, too, am a photographer of sorts. He tells us he is heading across to Ireland in search of old family roots, and he is in the midst of a three-month-long tour of Europe. We tell him that everyone has roots in Ireland, so he is bound to find someone to claim him. The bus pulls into the bowels of the ferry, and we disembark into the boat; bus passengers dispersing into the various staircases to access the passenger decks.

The ferry is busier than we are used to. Presumably, we are not the only ones heading home after the summer holiday. Others have clearly saved these last two weeks of the school holidays to cram in a trip to Ireland, and excited children run up and down the lounges, shouting and playing in the aisles. We find a quieter spot, away from the families, and spread ourselves across a cosy corner sofa with a window view over the Irish Sea. I pull out my book, my daughter her phone, for last precious moments of free wi-fi before we set sail. By the time we set sail, we are hemmed in with a huge family of

Germans spilling across our access paths out of our corner. Resigning myself easily to a non-eventful journey where I will choose not to leave my seat, I prop my feet on the sofa and recline onto my bag, pretending to read but really just dozing to the white noise of my neighbours talking intensely in a language I don't understand.

We are somewhere in the middle of the Irish Sea when my daughter kicks me awake and gestures across the aisle. Camera Man is there again.

"We should invite him to stay," she suggests. "He's really nice."

I pull myself into a sitting position to look across. He's drinking Guinness and already pretending to be a genuine Irishman returning home. Or a blatant tourist. I can't decide. I don't think he sees us, but I guess he's been up on the outside deck, taking pictures of his farewell to Wales and the UK. Something about him looks windswept and rugged, and I predict he will return to the deck in time to greet Ireland through his camera lens. I murmur something about not moving now to talk to him; the Germans are still blocking our way out, and I'm comfortable here. I placate her by agreeing that if we see him later, I'll ask him where he's staying and which part of Ireland he's heading to.

"Cool," she concedes and lays on the seat along from me, resting her head on my legs. Funny that she's so taken with this stranger.

When I sit upright again, as the captain announces our approach into Dublin, Camera Man is gone. So are the Germans, but we stay where we are until the ferry shudders to a final stop, engines off. Only when we are called to gather in the foot passengers' disembarkation areas, do we gather our bags and move.

"Remember to look for that man," my daughter reminds me, but I don't see him in the assembled group.

And then suddenly, he is beside us. It's easy enough to strike up conversation again, and he readily volunteers that his family research is bringing him within an hour of where we live. He has places to stay tonight and tomorrow night, but no definite arrangements for when he ventures out of Dublin later in the week.

"Come and stay," we say, meaning it. There is something in this stranger that I recognise—that I trust without question —and he seems like he is already a friend. We exchange contact details, noting again the similarities of our jobs. He is journaling his travels in his photographs, for an exhibition he has planned on his return home. Other passengers also seem pulled to his magnetic openness and are shamelessly eavesdropping as I offer suggestions for his journey to the midlands. Another couple adds their own suggestions, and a younger woman standing the other side of me mentions an exhibition he might like to see while he is in Dublin. A turbaned man standing near us produces a pen without being asked, as I grope in my bag and realise I don't have one. A faceless voice on the PA system directs us to begin our exit, and the crowd moves again. We are funnelled into the stairwells, losing Camera Man again.

CHAPTER FORTY-FOUR

IN THE BEGINNING

*I*t has been some months now since Camera Man left Ireland. He is somewhere else in Europe now, treading softly through other strangers' lives, taking snapshots of other places, other people, other stories. The impact he had on my life has lingered in his physical absence, and we keep in touch by messages and emails. He has made me reconsider some things I thought I knew, and I have a new sense of hope that mixes with the sense of loss that, once again, I have lost someone who feels as if he might have been important.

I am idly skimming through my phone when a link to a magazine article catches my attention. Intrigued by its headline and the beautiful arty photo accompanying it, I follow the link. Uncharacteristically, I read it to the end, transfixed and mesmerized. This is the story of the widely held Asian belief that invisible red threads stretch between people, forging unbreakable, constant connections to strangers who are really friends and soulmates. Some believe this to be a romantic link, a link to a lover. Others have a wider view, encompassing links between parents and children who have not yet been born, or siblings separated when too young to remember each other. Whatever the link, that thread may tangle, twist, or stretch, and take the connections through unpredictable paths, but will never break. I cannot shake the message of the article, and now the thoughts of the stranger I met on a ferry haunt my days, while Charles still visits my dreams.

I stalk Camera Man's Facebook—both business and personal—more intently after he leaves Ireland, looking for his story, and it doesn't take me long to realise I can read his pages as clearly as if they were my own. I guess from photos, comments, condolences, and the rush to leave his home to find answers, roots, and solace, that he, too, once had a business partner he had become too close to. I ask him, and I am right. In return, I tell him the basics of how I guessed his story, and I find I have opened up more to this stranger than to anyone in years. He reciprocates, and, once again, I know I know him, despite having met only fleetingly.

He stayed with us that week after we met on the ferry. I had a brief moment of self-doubt as to the sensibility of inviting a stranger into my home, of offering a bed to a man I didn't know while my teenage daughter slept in the next room, and while I, too, would sleep defenceless and unprotected, just a step across the landing from him. I wondered again why Jess had never returned, or if I should have found another dog to fill her empty space, to protect and reassure.

"What if he's an axe murderer?" I had asked my child, sharing the blame and the responsibility for having invited this stranger in.

"Ask him," she'd countered.

So I did. I'd already checked out his profile by then, as

soon as he had accepted the invitation, a few days after we'd
met. I'd emailed him once I'd gotten home from the ferry, to
confirm my offer was genuine, and to tell him he was
welcome to stay with us as he passed through the midlands.
He'd replied fast, that he was happy to come—a stranger
trusting a stranger, if we believe in face value. I wrote a quick
message, useless but necessary.

Just checking . . . Are you an axe murderer?
No, are you?
No.

And with that mutual, if futile, reassurance, and a
reminder to my daughter that it would only be a mistake we
could make once, we agreed he would come. Late on the
Friday evening of the same week, he arrived, a little later than
agreed after a mix up with hire cars and a let-down of sat nav
directions. Tired, hungry, but bearing the same easy
friendship we remembered from the ferry, I invited him
inside. We opened cold bottles of craft beers, ate an over-
cooked risotto, and sat in the garden in the fading sunlight of
that August evening. There, in gathering darkness, we talked
late into the night, about nothing I can remember now. He had
planned to move on the following day, driven onwards by a
need to find roots, family, connections, or anchors, but
instead, on that Saturday morning, my daughter cajoled him
into my car, and I drove him to photograph local landmarks,
wild areas of untamed bog, and the gothic ruins of an old
monastery. By the time the day was done, it was too late to
move on to a new place, and he stayed another night.

He left early the next morning, up and out just as dawn
broke. He had promised to slip away quietly, to not disturb; I
promised I'd get up to see him off, not really sure if I would
manage to wake in time. I should have slept lightly, with this
stranger in our house, but I was sleeping soundly when the

creaking of footsteps on the landing woke me, as he crept downstairs from the spare room. I made coffee while he gathered his things, then stood on the doorstep in my pyjamas to wave him goodbye. My daughter, too, had stumbled from her bed, not wanting to miss a final few minutes with our stranger-friend. We hugged at the door, holding on to each other as if to imprint a mutual reminder of the trust we'd placed in each other, and then he was gone.

Though the link to the red thread article has long disappeared into the archives of my search history, its message stays with me, tumbling around in my mind for days, which stretch into weeks, into months. Camera Man is home again, back on the far side of the world. I realise when I study my globe that he is almost exactly opposite to me, and a straight line through the centre of the earth would almost join us—mere centimetres apart but a world away. He is not sure how happy he is to be home, as now he must face the things he was running from. He tells me he's tired from his travels, but more exhausted from the things he must deal with now in order to move forward. I'm years ahead of him in this, and I share with him how hard it was to divide a business, a life, and a heart. We talk often, by messages either exchanged late in my evenings to coincide with him waking and starting his day, or vice versa—snatched time in my mornings as I rush between waking and readying myself for a working day, while he winds down and heads into sleep time. I can tell when he is feeling low and needs a friend, and although we only met for three days, divided into a short meeting of strangers on one boat trip home and a two day stay when one stranger put trust in another and realised they knew each other well enough to believe in each other, he opens up to me, and we share our biggest secrets and our fears and our sadnesses. We also share happy moments and non-news and snippets of each other's upward climb as we stay determined to become who we know we can become. We sometimes don't communicate for several weeks, or months pass by, but then one will text just as the other was thinking about them as the red thread tightens between us, pulling our souls together despite oceans of distance.

As another winter draws in and my days begin to darken, I make a decision that I share with no one. My children are away, in their own lives. James, who I speak to far less often now the children are grown, is happy with his new life, and I am happy for him. He looks well, and the haggard despair I had painted on his face has left him. He has found someone who loves him enough and puts him first. He is busy with work, having been promoted more than once, and things are good for him. I don't miss him anymore. I have learned to evict the biggest spiders and change fuses without his help, and despite our two decades of marriage, I am usually happy alone and enjoy my own company. But now . . . now, I am finally ready for something new.

I feel only excitement and anticipation as I wait at my gate, checking over and over that I have my passport, my boarding pass, and my currency. Announcements crackle in the air around me; people come and go. I don't know how my story will end, or where it will go, but I have decided how it will start. I am certain that when I arrive unannounced at his gallery, or at his front door, or wherever he is when I find him, he will welcome me as I welcomed him. I don't know where he lives, but I know the invisible red thread that has been persistently tugging at me since it first tied us together will take me to him. What I find there will help me decide my future. I know he will put me up for at least the reciprocal 'stay for a night or two,' whatever his own situation is now. It's been a few months since we last spoke, and I don't know if he is alone. There have been passing—usually fleeting— relationships for us both since we met, but I have found no one who pulls at me strongly enough to commit to. Whatever his situation, I know he will be as pleased to see me as I was when he came to stay with me. I will stay for a night, or a few nights, and then I will move on, to travel alone and enjoy the adventure, or … or I will stay for a few nights, and then I will stay for some more.

A flight attendant in a uniform embellished with the red-gold insignia of the airline announces the gate is open. Through the window, I see a motif of flame-like feathers painted on the plane's tail. I retrieve my boarding pass and passport, and join the queue for boarding.

The End.
(Or a new beginning . . .)

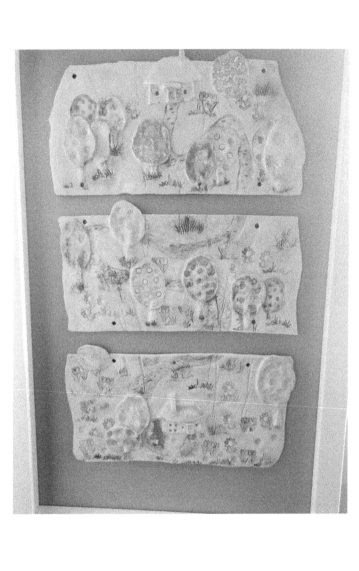

AUTHOR'S NOTE

The ceramic artwork pictured is called *Inevitable Pathway* and was created by the author during the same period that she was working on *Dear Isobel.*

Inevitable Pathway is one of a set of linked pieces. The complete set of three depicts the idea that the paths we take, or that the decisions we make in life, all lead to the same place. Each of the artworks show a small, red-cloaked girl setting out from the same cottage at the base of the piece. In each of the artworks, she is following a pathway through the forest to the same ultimate destination: the cottage at the top of the piece. The other two pieces depict the same figure, but faced with either a random tangle of pathways to meander along *(Random Pathway),* or a choice of only two directions *(Chosen Pathway).*

In *Inevitable Pathway,* there is only one pathway for each figure to take. She *will* walk *that* path and reach *that* destination.

My publisher and I selected this artwork for inclusion here for its portrayal of the narrator's increasing certainty that whatever choices she made in her life, the outcome would have been the same. Within *Dear Isobel,* the narrator relates how she believes the affair was both 'inevitable and unstoppable', although she is less certain of this in an earlier letter to Isobel: *'And I don't know if the inevitable then happened, or if is wasn't inevitable at all and we could've stopped it'.*

We would love to hear what readers think. Are our lives pre-destined and set, or can we alter our course by the decisions we make?

Book Club Questions for Dear Isobel

1. What is the significance of the title? Did you find it meaningful, why or why not?
2. Would you have given the book a different title? If yes, what would your title be?
3. What were the main themes of the book? How were those themes brought to life?
4. Were there any quotes (or passages) that stood out to you? Why?
5. What did you like most about the book? What did you like the least?
6. How did the book make you feel? What emotions did it evoke?
7. What do you think the author's goal was in writing this book? What ideas were they trying to illustrate? What message were they trying to send?
8. What did you learn from this book?
9. Did this book remind you of any other books that you've read? Describe the connection.
10. Did your opinion of this book change as you read it? How?
11. Would you recommend the book to a friend? How would you summarize the story if you were to recommend it?
12. If you could talk to the author, what burning question would you want to ask?
13. Which character did you most relate to and why?
14. Which character or moment prompted the strongest emotional reaction for you? Why?
15. One early reader described the narrator of this

book as 'deeply dislikeable'. To what extent do you agree with this observation of her?

16. What motivates the actions of each of the characters in the book?

17. Do you think that the narrator sent any of the letters and text messages to Isobel, or were they all only sent and received in her imagination?

18. The narration of this story is clearly unreliable, and we never get to hear Isobel's point of view, except in the letters (which may or may not have been figments of the narrator's imagination.) How much sympathy did you feel towards Isobel, and how much of the narrator's side of the story do you think she would understand?

19. Did you feel sympathy or empathy with the main character? Did her first person account make it easier to relate to her circumstances? If she had been named, or had the story been told from a third person point of view, do you think this would have created more distance and lessened any empathy or sympathy towards her?

20. If the book were made into a movie, who would play each of the lead characters?

21. What scene would you point out as the pivotal moment in the narrative? How did it make you feel?

22. What scene resonated with you most on a personal level? Why? How did it make you feel?

23. What surprised you most about the book? Why? What was your favourite chapter and why?

24. Have any of your personal views changed because of this book? If so, how?

25. Did you think the story was believable or too

farfetched? How did you feel about the ending?
How might you change it?

26. Did you ever consider that Charles would leave
Isobel and make a go of things with the narrator?
Were you surprised that James stayed around for
so long after the affair came to light? Or that
Charles and Isobel stayed together? Discuss.

27. What songs did you think of while reading this
book? (For extra fun: make a playlist!) Please turn
the page for Jinny Alexander's own playlist for
Dear Isobel.

Jinny's playlist for Dear Isobel. Strictly in order!

1. I'm Not in Love, 10cc
    2. Distance, Christina Perri ft. Jason Mraz
    3. America, Razorlight
    4. Ever Fallen in Love, Gemma Hayes *cover version*
    5. Chasing Cars, Snow Patrol
    6. Saving All My Love For You, Whitney Houston
    7. Wire to Wire, Razorlight
    8. Tell Her About It, Billy Joel
    9. Sound of Silence, Disturbed *cover version*
    10. Miles, Christina Perri
    11. Believe it, New Model Army
    12. Lonely, Christina Perri
    13. Lean on me, Bill Withers
    14. Poison Street, New Model Army

ACKNOWLEDGMENTS

Thank you first, to you: the person who is still reading. Thank you for reading *Dear Isobel*.

After that, my biggest thanks must go to my husband, who has supported me and *most* of the decisions I have made in our life together. He is wonderful, and appreciated more than I usually tell him.

Thank you to my son and my daughter for their support and encouragement to put this book out into the world. And to my son for tech support.

Thank you to those who shared their stories. When I started to write this, even the most basic internet search told me that 1 in 4 people in relationships experience infidelity. And that, presumably, are just those who admit to it. When I began talking to people, I realised that it is more common than anyone cares to admit. It's not always an easy thing to talk about, especially if you are the Isobel or the James in the situation. It is you I thank here. I also thank those who talked to me about their experiences in the narrator's shoes. I chose to keep her nameless, because she represents all of you. Thank you for baring your souls to me.

Thank you to my early readers, without whom I would have probably given up. Your feedback and cheerleading and recognition for the story powered me on. The kindness of friends and strangers who read and took time to give me feedback is not forgotten.

Thank you to my wider family. I mention you here because I know you will recognise the scenes in the chapter entitled Two Weeks Away. I wanted to immortalise that holiday—it was mostly kind of fun, wasn't it?

Thank you to my publisher and the team at Creative James Media for sharing my belief that *Dear Isobel* is a story that needed to be shared with the world.

Thank you Steve for giving me a story to use for the ending; the introduction to Mel, and the feet.

Huge thanks to my two wonderful photographer friends:

Melany Hunt at *Le Toi Photography and Digital Arts* www.letoi.co.nz for the cover photos.

Shelley Corcoran at *Shelley Corcoran Photography* http://www.shelleycorcoran-photography.com for my author photos.

And again, to you, thank you for reading.

9 781735 392615